Totally Bound Publishing books by Kait Gamble:

Cuffed

The Long Way Round
Grind
Ignite
Scorch

Totally Five Star
Breaking Rossi's Rules
Fuel to the Fire

Totally Five Star: St. Lucia

FUEL TO THE FIRE

KAIT GAMBLE

Fuel to the Fire
ISBN # 978-1-78430-963-3
©Copyright Kait Gamble 2016
Cover Art by Posh Gosh ©Copyright January 2016
Interior text design by Claire Siemaszkiewicz
Totally Bound Publishing

Published in 2016 by Totally Bound Publishing, Newland House, The Point, Weaver Road, Lincoln, LN6 3QN, United Kingdom.

FUEL TO THE FIRE

Dedication

For our first loves.

Chapter One

Jackie got out of the cab and took a moment to stare at the magnificent hotel. Right away just gazing at the building, she knew that her stay here would be something different. Instead of towering into the sky, the hotel sprawled up the mountainside and outward to the limits of her peripheral vision. The stone façade might as well have been hewn from the rock face while the lush greenery threatened to envelop the entire thing and reclaim it for Mother Nature. The hotel appeared so incredibly natural it could have been a part of the mountain itself.

On the other side, clear blue water lapped at immaculate white sand dotted with brilliant vermillion umbrellas and wooden loungers she couldn't wait to try out.

Magnificent.

In a slight daze, she walked into the grand foyer and out of the sultry air to take a deep breath of the chilled, perfumed interior. Her kitten heels clicked along the stone floor as she gazed at the beautiful architecture and design. The abundance of stone and wood gave the space an organic feel. Dominating one of the walls, a waterfall splashed, surrounded by indigenous plants and a pool where colorful fish flashed in the water. Together with the enormous windows and natural light, the room exuded the perfect relaxed island ambience.

It felt good—great—to be somewhere different. She couldn't remember the last time she'd been on a trip anywhere, let alone somewhere so opulent.

"Jackie! You made it!"

A slender, elegant blonde figure dashed toward her. She was quickly engulfed by the well-toned arms of her best friend, Caroline.

She hugged her friend back. It had been too long. Jackie stepped away to smile at Caroline. "Of course. You didn't think I would skip out on your wedding, did you?"

"It never crossed my mind." Brilliant green eyes sparkling, she wound her arm through Jackie's and led her through the hotel. "Ever been here?"

Jackie grinned up at the luxurious surroundings and shook her head. "No. it's always been on the bucket list, though." The beautifully lush island of St. Lucia was the complete opposite of her everyday life.

Caroline grinned. "I'm glad." Her smile softened. "It really is wonderful to see you. Things haven't been the same without you."

A pang of emotion Jackie didn't want to name twinged in her chest. The first of many times this weekend, she was sure. "Things have been a bit different, haven't they?"

"Head's up." Caroline nodded, her attention on someone behind Jackie.

Jackie had a fraction of a second to brace herself before the group of women was upon them.

"Jaqueline Pennington! I thought it was you!" Regina, Caroline's mother, sashayed up to Jackie with her arms out swept. But instead of a hug, she clasped her by the shoulders and air-kissed her at each cheek. She stepped back to give her a critical once-over, making Jackie glad she had primped at the airport before getting in the cab. Though, from the thinly veiled disapproval in the woman's eyes, Jackie didn't quite make the cut. "My, you *have* changed! They have a spa here that's supposed to work wonders."

Ignoring the last comment, Jackie flipped her ponytail over her shoulder as she forced herself to smile at the well-coiffed woman and her friends. "It has been a few years, hasn't it? They *have* been kind to you, haven't they?" Not enough, by Jackie's reckoning. "We should go to the spa together and have a nice long chat and really catch up."

The older woman's expression grew pinched at the insinuation that she would need such a long session, but she quickly recovered. "We're all so glad you're here." She looped Jackie's arm through hers and started walking.

Caroline gave her a helpless shrug and a pleading smile. It was her friend's wedding weekend, and Jackie refused to do anything that would ruin it.

"I saw your mother just the other day. She's doing well. She tells me that she and your father are heading to Rome this summer."

All the muscles in her body contracted at the mention of her parents. She'd known someone would bring them up sooner or later, but she'd hoped it would have taken longer than five minutes after she arrived. "That's nice," Jackie said as mildly as she could.

"It is. They've done quite a bit of traveling, from what I've heard."

Jackie really had no comment about that, so she stayed silent. Focusing on the scenery was much more interesting than listening to Regina blather on about her parents.

"Mum, it's been a while since Jackie and I have seen each other. I wanted to spend some time together before everything starts."

Regina slowed to a stop. "Yes, of course! Silly me!" She spun Jackie into Caroline's arms. "Dinner is at eight." And with that, she flitted off leaving a thick wake of Chanel No. 5.

They watched her until they were sure she was out of earshot.

Caroline smiled apologetically. "Sorry about that. Mum didn't think you would come, and I don't think she quite knows what to say."

Regina hadn't been the only one not to know if she was going to make it. "It's fine. I doubt I'd know what to say either."

Her friend didn't look convinced. "You know, if money is a problem, my offer to pay for your stay still stands."

How had she managed to have such a good friend? "Thanks. But I'm okay—at least for the moment." She laughed weakly. "I highly doubt I'll make use of the magical spa they have here, though."

Caroline joined her in her mirth. "It can't be that great. Otherwise, Mum would never leave it."

Jackie inhaled the fragrant air again and felt her muscles slowly unknot. It had been a long flight and she'd been tense worrying about the kind of reception she'd get. She had expected an inquisition, so she was relieved at how things had fared so far.

She had an entire week to make it through yet.

Caroline led her to the reception and stood by as Jackie went through the formality of checking in.

"We had a minor disaster thanks to one of the groomsmen getting into a skiing accident last week. Charles assures me that he's found a suitable replacement and that he will be here today so you won't have to walk down the aisle alone."

The last thing she was worried about was walking down the aisle solo. "It's lucky you found someone on such short notice." Jackie barely remembered the days when she could drop everything at a moment's notice to do whatever she liked.

Jackie was dimly aware of masculine voices heading toward them. Two of them sounded familiar. She knew Caroline's fiancé, Charles. They'd met a few times before. A Sutcliffe through and through, he was tall, broad, golden blond and blessed with a knack for finances like the rest of his dynasty. It was his laugh that she was able to pick up on immediately.

But the other voice…

The hairs on the back of her neck slowly stood to attention as it dawned on her whose voice was pricking her memory.

Palms growing slick, she turned to find the groom and what appeared to be his groomsmen gathered around them.

Charles and Caroline made a striking couple. Both beautiful and golden, they looked like they belonged on the cover of a magazine. He wrapped his arms around his fiancée and the gazes between them could only be described as blissful.

But Jackie's attention was torn away to focus on the darkly handsome man next to him. He still had the same rangy build she remembered, but he had filled out in a way that made her hands itch with want to touch him—to explore. He looked more refined, though just barely. The worn T-shirts and jeans that she knew he had favored in the past were replaced by khakis and a white button-down. The garment's rolled-up sleeves revealed sculpted forearms. His clothes contrasted with his tan skin and slightly wild, dark hair and penetrating eyes. Logan Forrester looked dangerous—and angry.

Jackie, by contrast, was tired and rumpled from the flight and she knew everyone could see it. It wasn't something that could be hidden by her quick change into some of the few designer items she still owned and a haphazard makeup retouch before leaving the airport.

The moment their eyes, met she couldn't help the onslaught of memories that flooded her mind.

What was Logan doing here?

Fury and confusion mixed potently in her blood as she stared at him. Jackie couldn't break his hypnotic gaze. He looked just as surprised to see her, but he quickly recovered. His eyes darkened impossibly as he raked his contemplative regard over her.

Jackie caught Caroline's panicked eye before she turned to her fiancé. "What's going on?"

"This is the tech genius I was telling you about, and my new groomsman." Charles' smile never wavered. "Lucky for us, he just happened to be here on business. What a coincidence, isn't it?"

Quite.

Jackie's lungs seized. It was as if she'd stepped outside her own body to watch the seriously horrifying situation. Yet, all she could do was stare at the devastatingly handsome man. The one she would never forget as long as she lived. She didn't wait for introductions and blurted out his name before she could give in to her impulse to put as much space between them as physically possible. Preferably at least a continent.

"Logan." His name came out as an indictment.

His smile stayed on his lips as he calmly greeted her with an equally icy, "Jackie."

The group around them quieted and stood back to watch them glare at each other. They would have fled a mile if they'd known the true depth of the feelings festering there.

Out of everyone there, only Caroline knew about her and Logan's turbulent parting. To the rest of them, it probably looked like two old lovers meeting again, awkwardly. An explosive combination that would inevitably detonate. All they needed to do was wait and watch for amusement. If only it were something so simple.

Her friend shoved her fiancé off with a glare before grabbing Jackie and her suitcase to drag them both away.

Caroline stomped along for several tense seconds before she growled, "I had no idea he was here, Jackie. I swear."

Still dazed and too numb to care, Jackie nodded.

She'd never thought she would see Logan again. She had put him out of her mind years ago, refusing to think about him or the decision that had changed the course of her entire life.

He had disappeared not too long after he'd graduated from university.

After asking her to marry him.

After she had dropped everything to be with him.

It was completely surreal. She couldn't get her mind around the fact that Logan Forrester had come crashing back into her life.

Chapter Two

Logan watched Jackie get hauled away by Caroline. Wasn't that just a flashback of old times? Caroline never had liked him. The uppity heiress had always thought he was beneath them. It figured a stuck-up girl like her wouldn't look twice at a guy like him.

But Jackie had.

He hadn't seen her since the night he'd graduated. The night he'd thought would be the beginning of a new life for them both. The night Jackie had kicked him in the teeth and told him to take a hike, when she had realized he wasn't good enough for her.

Logan knew he should just walk away from the whole situation, but he'd promised to help Charles. Not to mention, she looked damn good. Still as prim and proper as ever. Her chestnut hair was longer, but was tugged back in a ponytail like she always used to do — something her mother had hated, or so Jackie had told him. At least she hadn't buckled under the pressure her parents piled on her to look and act how they thought she should. She still wore designer clothing, dragged a suitably labeled suitcase, but she looked different. But then why wouldn't she? It had been years since they'd seen each other. She would hardly be the girl in her late teens that he remembered. What he did know was that underneath the polished beauty was a sensual woman.

He wondered if *that* Jackie was still there.

The thought sent blood straight to his groin. He hated how his body responded to mere memories of her. After the way Jackie treated him, the last woman he should want was her. But incredibly enough, he did.

Damn her and damn his cock.

The chemistry between them had been blistering, explosive. The sex, even more so. Was it any wonder his body craved her? There had been other women here and there, but they had all paled in comparison to Jackie. They had been tools to slake his lust and none had managed to get under his skin the way she had. As much as he hated to admit it, she had been the love of his life.

And she had disposed of him like an empty coffee cup.

He watched the sway of her hips—her ass—as she walked away, further fueling his memories and sending more blood to his cock—pissing him off even more.

The shock in her eyes when she'd seen him was real, as was the anger. She'd been angry to see him? What reason did she have to be mad? She had been the one to drop him when he no longer fit into her neat little life.

But there was something else under the fury. Pain?

If anyone should feel pain at that moment it was him.

However, the thought of her suffering in his presence sparked a merciless little impulse in the back of his mind. Why shouldn't he make her hurt? She had devastated him. And all because he wasn't rich enough or of the proper breeding. He might not have been able to do anything about his parentage, but he was now one of the richest men on the planet, even topping the paltry fortune her family had been so proud of.

A fact he would love to rub in her face.

He turned to Charles, only to realize that they were all watching him avidly. "What?" He snarled.

"Wow. I'd ask if you two know each other, but it's obvious. Just like the fact that you dislike each other." Charles cocked his head with a shit-eating grin. "Bad breakup?"

"You could say that." Logan got the feeling that the man wasn't privy to the details of their relationship and he was going to keep it that way. The last thing he needed was the news of how she'd dumped him spreading through the wedding party.

"It's not going to be a problem, is it?" Charles eyed him critically.

"We're not going to do anything to ruin your wedding." No, it wasn't going to be a problem for him.

He would make sure it was going to be a problem for *her*, though.

* * * *

"Really, I'll be fine." Jackie must have said it at least five times, but Caroline actually seemed to take notice this time around.

Her friend fluttered to one end of the room and back as she paced aggravated lines. "Are you sure? I'll go tell Charles to get rid of him right now if you want."

"I can handle it." The last thing Jackie wanted was for her friend to get all bent out of shape when she was supposed to be celebrating a huge moment in her life. Though, watching her now, Jackie wasn't sure if it was too late to worry about that. "I can't let you upset your wedding plans yet again on my account." Surely, he wouldn't be able to stay here too long. She could barely afford two nights in the luxurious hotel. The week she had booked had taken a lot of creative meal planning and skipping out on the few luxuries she allowed herself in the months leading up to the trip... And probably would for a few months to follow.

"I want to kick his ass for you," Caroline fumed.

"You can't afford to ruin your nails." Jackie chuckled. "I'll be fine."

Caroline studied her eyes for a second before she nodded. "Right. But say the word and I'll have him removed from the hotel."

"Thanks."

"How can you be so calm?"

Is that how she looked? Inside, she was a seething, confused mess. Seeing him again had brought back too many feelings all at once, and Jackie had no idea what to do with them or how to vent.

"I'm not, really. But I'll be fine." The words sounded absurd even as she repeated them.

Caroline narrowed her eyes. "You keep saying that like you're trying to convince yourself."

She probably was. At the moment, Jackie felt as though she was a completely disassociated bystander just witnessing things unfold.

"I honestly don't know what I'm feeling," She sighed. How could she explain the molten mass of confusion?

"You're in shock." Caroline wrapped an arm around Jackie's shoulders and rubbed her bare arm. "Come on. Let's get some drinks. Then go down to dinner."

With a sigh, Jackie got up and kicked at her small, worn Louis Vuitton suitcase. "I need to freshen up." Not that it would matter, since nothing she'd brought with her was anywhere near the quality that everyone else would be wearing.

"Do you want to borrow anything of mine?" Caroline offered helpfully.

Jackie gave her friend an exasperated glance. "You're kidding, right? We might have been the same size once upon a time. But now?" She waved at herself.

Over the past few years she'd gained a few pounds. Nothing excessive, but it was enough to make her self-conscious. She was no longer the slender beauty that Caroline still was. Work had taken over most of her life and it left her too exhausted to do anything but search for ways to relax.

Caroline gaped at her. "Don't be ridiculous. You're gorgeous."

Jackie rolled her eyes. "Please."

Caroline mimicked the move in a more exaggerated way. "If it'll make you feel better, I'll bring my makeup and hair stuff. Or, better yet, we can hit the spa and have the staff give you a bit of a makeover to boost your confidence."

That did sound great. Jackie couldn't remember the last time someone else had done her hair and makeup. "It's tempting."

"It's settled." Caroline had already picked up the phone and started making the arrangements. In only a few minutes, her friend had her hustling down the hall toward the spa.

Jackie dug her heels in. "I can't afford it. I can barely handle being here in the first place."

Caroline waved her concerns away. "It's my treat. Now shut up and let me do this for you."

Her friend had a slightly maniacal look on her face that pinged an alarm in the back of her mind. "Why are you really doing this?" Was it because she wasn't up to par with her other bridesmaids? "I'm sorry if I don't look as good as the other girls in your party, but—"

Caroline's green eyes rounded incredulously. "I keep telling you, you look amazing."

Jackie shook her head. "So why do you look like you're on a mission?"

Caroline clenched her free hand into a fist. "Because I am. I'm going to make you so drool-worthy that Logan will swallow his tongue when he sees you again."

Jackie yanked her arm out of her friend's grasp. "That's what this is all about?"

"Yes."

Jackie almost laughed at the feverish glint that sparked in her friend's eyes. "I don't care what he thinks of me."

She gripped Jackie's shoulders. "Yes, you do. And we're going to make him wish he never took off on you. Then you're going to be the one to destroy *him*."

That did have a poetic ring to it. To be the one to tear out Logan's heart would be so satisfying… But she shoved the idea aside. "I don't want to go down that route again. The man's toxic and the further we stay away from him, the better."

"Well, you do have to walk with him down the aisle… Unless I rework the line-up for you…" Jackie could see her friend file away the thought for later. "We just want him to see you and kick himself for ever letting you go."

"That does sound appealing." What could it hurt? It wasn't like she gave a damn about how he felt. She would give him a taste of what he'd been missing out on then she'd get on with her life.

The triumphant smile lit up Caroline's face. "Of course it does. Plus it will give me something to do other than obsess over the wedding."

That definitely sounded good. The last thing she needed was for Caroline to worry herself sick over what was sure to be a perfect wedding.

Jackie sighed and relented. "Okay, then. But nothing over the top."

Caroline grinned. "That's the spirit!" Grabbing Jackie's hand, she bounded the rest of the way to the spa.

* * * *

It took a couple of hours and half a glass of champagne for Jackie, and three for Caroline, but by the time the team at the spa stepped back with satisfied smiles, Jackie felt like a new person.

Regina had been right. The spa was amazing. Jackie stared at her reflection. She was as bright and shiny as a new penny. After a masterful facial and a full body mud pack, her skin had regained a healthy glow that she hadn't seen in ages, while her hair shone in the light, thanks to the magical concoction that had been smeared into it. A manicure and pedicure had rounded out the session. Jackie felt and smelled amazing.

"That's the smile I'm looking for." Caroline eyed Jackie critically as she circled her.

"You know that's kind of creepy when you do that when I'm standing here in just a robe."

Her friend waggled a finger at her before pressing it to her lips in thought. "Hush. I'm just trying to figure out if there's anything else we need to do."

"I think they've done just about all they can do." Jackie looked at herself in the mirror. "It's a miracle."

Caroline didn't respond. Instead, she ran her fingers through the ends of Jackie's chestnut hair. "You should go a bit shorter."

Jackie snatched her hair back. "Is a bit one inch or ten?"

"I'm not saying you need to get scalped. Just some shaping."

Murmurs of agreement came from the small group.

"Fine. But I don't want to lose too much." And she narrowed her eyes at Caroline. "And I'm paying for the cut."

From the grin on her face, her friend was just happy to get her way.

Jackie let them lead her to a chair, her heart feeling lighter than it had in a long time.

* * * *

It was amazing how much a few hours at the spa could change her outlook on life — on herself. Her spirits at a euphoric high, she grinned at herself in the mirror.

She'd let Caroline buy her one outfit, at her insistence. Jackie would make sure to pay her back in other ways to salve her conscience.

Caroline did have exquisite taste. The floaty, sleeveless, silk swing dress was perfect for the tropical atmosphere. Dressed up with a long gold necklace, strappy sandals and her new hair, she looked glamorous enough for a meal with society types. At least she could pretend to fit in with them for a while. This one meal, to be precise. Afterward, the outfit would be unfit for any other event during this trip lest she become even more of a point of ridicule.

She pushed that thought aside. What she relished was the prospect of making Logan regret his decision to walk out on her.

The thought of having to have a meal with him took a little of the shine out her eyes. Jackie had never imagined she would see him again. She would never admit it aloud, but in the year just after he'd disappeared, she had done a quick search or two online for him, but nothing had ever come up. Once she'd gotten it out of her system, Jackie had refused to waste any more time on a man who obviously didn't give a damn about her.

So why did she care what she looked like to him tonight?

Jackie kicked her open suitcase and watched it skid across the floor. It would be so easy to just stay hidden in the suite. It was huge and beautiful, and she could happily stay ensconced within it until the wedding, and afterward until it was time to leave.

Caroline would be disappointed, though. Jackie couldn't do that to her oldest friend. Not to mention, she couldn't let a trip like this go to waste. Who knew when she would get another vacation like this one?

She'd flown all the way out here and had been prepared to deal with the condescending comments and snide remarks. What was one more thing to endure?

Jackie put on a confident smile and brushed her now gleaming hair over her shoulder. He wouldn't know what had hit him. None of them would.

Chapter Three

Logan smiled wanly as he sat listening to yet another mind-numbing anecdote about someone's car, or dog, or something. There was no way he could get his mind to focus on the drivel that was coming out of these people's mouths. Not only was it completely uninteresting to him, but he could not stop thinking about Jackie.

The years hadn't changed her much. She was just as beautiful as ever. The emotion in her eyes when she saw him, however... That was *very* different.

He had seen a myriad of emotions pass over her face in that fleeting moment. There had been anger, most definitely — that had been at the forefront — but behind it he was sure he'd seen sadness — devastation, even. What the hell did she have to be that upset about? She had been the one to instigate their breakup.

And anger? *He* was the one who should feel both.

Wanting to get to the bottom of everything, Logan made sure he would be there for the meal, though he had planned to be 'busy' for most of the festivities unless absolutely necessary.

These people weren't his friends or family. He was simply doing a guy a favor. That was until Jackie had been added to the equation. She definitely gave this week a more interesting turn.

He forced himself to join in when he heard the collective laughter from all around him. Might as well make some effort to fit in while he was there. And if he was going to be spending any amount of time with the group, it was better not to stick out any more than he already did.

His chuckle died when his gaze fell on Jackie, who had just appeared at the entrance to the restaurant.

Her wide-eyed glance at the room and the way she clenched and unclenched her hands at her sides were a red flag that she was uncomfortable, even dreading being there. Was that because of him?

As far as he could tell, she hadn't even seen him yet.

Logan continued to watch her.

Obviously recovered from her flight, Jackie presented a stunning figure in that little dress. It showed off her long, shapely legs to fantastic effect. Her hair gleamed in the low light, adding to the glow that seemed to surround her. He witnessed her transformation from timid bunny to fierce tigress as she swept her hair over her shoulder. She straightened her spine and put a smile on her face as she strode in.

He bit his lip, forcing back the urge to go over, pick her up and take her to his room. It was just the lighting—his hormones. It was amazing what the right clothes, hair and makeup could do.

Logan clenched his fists and forced himself to look away.

"Jackie!" Caroline's mother smiled hugely when she saw Jackie. The woman immediately swooped, as if Jackie was the most important lady in the room. "You look wonderful, dear. Didn't I tell you a little time at the spa would work miracles?"

The woman's snide comment rankled him. What the hell was *that* supposed to mean? He might not have any claim on Jackie, but he knew she was the most striking woman in the restaurant. She could have been dragged backward through bushes and worn a sack and would still have been miles prettier than all the other women present. Unless she wanted to make a dig at Jackie because she made her and Caroline look like a couple of hags?

He kept his mouth shut as the harridan made an outrageous fuss over Jackie before ushering her over to the empty seat next to Logan.

"We thought pairing the couples who are to walk down the aisle together would be a good idea so that you could all get to know each other a little better." Regina practically frog-marched Jackie to the seat. He was sure that if Jackie hadn't sat as easily as she had, the old woman would have kicked her legs out from under her.

The waft of a scent that came from Jackie shot straight to his groin and had him shifting in his seat. The delicate aroma of her mingled with a lightly floral perfume and it made his mouth water.

"Hi." Jackie barely even looked at him as she settled into her seat.

"Hey."

Logan saw her catch Caroline's attention as she entered with Charles. Her friend's eyes widened when she saw them together. She raised her eyebrows at Jackie, who shrugged minutely, and he knew there was some sort of silent communication passing between the two women.

So she was stuck seated next to him. So what? Was she so revolted by him that she couldn't even stand sitting there?

He shifted and accidentally touched her foot with his. Jackie jolted as if he'd wound up and kicked her.

What the hell?

Jackie refused to look at him. Whenever conversation came her way, she would answer politely, but she seemed as uninterested in it all as he was.

So what was she doing here? He supposed her loyalty to Caroline was what had compelled her to fly over. Or perhaps she was in need of a new place to vacation?

His thoughts screeched to a halt as she played with her napkin. It had been rolled up like a tube and secured with an intricately carved wooden ring.

That she was sliding up and down unconsciously.

As if it was a cock. *His* cock.

Memories of her little hand wrapped around him choked his next breath. Logan ran his thumb over his brow as blood instantly shot south. Did she realize what she was doing? Was she teasing him on purpose?

If she was, two could play at that game.

Jackie shifted her knee away from Logan's for the umpteenth time. Of course she would have to be seated next to him. She took solace in the fact that at least, with him at her side, she didn't have to look at his face.

Not that she needed to see him to know that he was watching her. Jackie sensed his gaze on her skin as if he'd reached out and touched her.

His knee grazed hers again. Jackie glanced at him, and he shrugged as if he couldn't help what he was doing.

She stabbed the artichoke-baked brie with her fork and carved into it viciously. Then she nearly dropped her knife when his arm grazed hers. The contact was light—just a brush—but she might as well have stuck the knife in a power socket.

The conversation from around the table faded away—not that she was paying too much attention to what was being said. She didn't care about so-and-so's new car, or who was going to be wintering in Gstaad. Even less did she care about who had booked a seat on the Virgin Galactic for the first flight into space or someone's cousin's friend's misaligned new nose.

What she couldn't ignore was the heat coming from the man next to her. Or the scent of his cologne. Or the fact that she hated him, but for some insane reason wanted to climb on top of him and rip his clothes off right there in front of everyone.

Jackie gritted her teeth and attacked another slice of baked brie. Logan was the only man who'd ever made her lose control. And, as a result, lose her mind. She had fallen for every line he'd given her. Every stupid story and lie. All because they were compatible in bed.

So *very* compatible.

Sex with Logan was everything she'd ever dreamed and more. The kind of thing she'd read of in romance novels with all the fireworks that TV and movies made seem commonplace. It wasn't until she had dated other men that she'd realized the chemistry that she and Logan shared wasn't so easy to come by.

But she wasn't about to be an idiot for the second time. Jackie was older, wiser. She now knew the difference between good sex and love. Not that she'd had much experience with the latter. Or any at all, for that matter.

Sullenly, she glared at her food. It all looked so beautiful, and she was sure Caroline had agonized over every tiny detail, but she just couldn't enjoy any of it.

So she stared at the immense cylindrical aquarium the dining room circled like a donut. The water rippled with sunlight from above, lighting up the rainbow-colored coral and fish. Jackie loved the blue glow it gave the room. It was almost as if they were dining in an enchanted grotto deep below the waves.

Jackie swallowed and did her best to mold her expression into something neutral. Taking a slow breath, she tried again, this time taking a bite of a *chèvre* devil and attempted mentally to break it down into its ingredients as a way of passing the time. The sweetness of the date burst over her tongue and the goat's cheese gave it a tang before the candied pecan added complexity to the combined flavors. *Delicious.* She chewed appreciatively just as a question floated over the table to her.

"Jacqueline, Regina tells me you're a Pennington," said a dry, feminine voice.

She nearly choked on her appetizer as she let her gaze slide over to the woman speaking. Jackie recognized her as Caroline's aunt from photos her friend had shown her before. She smiled blithely as she replied, "I am."

Caroline waved her hand in front of the woman in a blatant attempt at distraction. "Have you seen my ring, Aunt Esther? Isn't it gorgeous?"

The woman nodded, pushing her hand away, completely undeterred. "Yes, it's fetching, but I'm interested in *her*." She peered at Jackie over her glasses. "Such a lovely young thing."

Jackie caught movement from the corner of her eye and looked over as Logan put his fork down and gazed at the woman levelly. "Is referring to a woman as if she's an object of curiosity how you people do things?"

Well, that answered the question of whether or not he still had his devil-may-care attitude. His temper was obviously still intact as well.

Everyone else joined Jackie in staring at Logan. She kicked his foot in an attempt to make him shut up. He didn't even flinch.

Esther puffed up, turning red as if she was going to explode. "And who are you?"

"Logan Forrester," he announced proudly.

"I don't know any Forresters."

"You wouldn't." Logan wiped his mouth then dropped the napkin as he turned to Charles and Caroline. "Thank you for the nice meal, but I have some calls to make that I'd forgotten about."

Then, inexplicably, he grabbed Jackie's arm and dragged her along behind him.

Horrified, Jackie gave her friend a pleading look before they rounded the corner and stepped out of sight.

"Let me go!" Jackie wrenched her hand from his grip only for him to grab her again and tighten his hold on her. "How could you do that? Wait. *Why* would you do that? You just ruined the meal and made a complete ass of yourself—and me!"

He looked at her with eyes filled with disdain. "You want to go back and let them talk about you like you're not even there? Go right ahead, princess."

She flinched at his use of his former nickname for her. "Don't call me that."

He faced her then. Stopped dead in the middle of the hall and zeroed in on her as if she was his prey. He stepped forward, forcing her to jerk back to keep the distance between them. Unfortunately, Jackie backed into a wall and trapped herself.

Logan pressed his hands against the wall on either side of her head, caging her. "You used to love it when I called you that."

She used to love a lot of things he did. No longer. Jackie glared up at him. "You're in my space."

"Another thing you used to love."

She shoved at his shoulders, but it was like trying to move a brick wall. Jackie's brain misfired the moment her fingers came into contact his hard body. It took far too long for her to remember she didn't want him there. Touching her. Overwhelming her senses.

She shoved again. "A lot has changed, Logan."

"I should say so." He let his gaze rove over her, lazily taking in every inch of her. "You look good." His attention wandered lower, settling on her pelvis. "Delicious, even."

Heat flared where his gaze settled. What was wrong with her?

"You're a pig." Naked under his scrutiny, Jackie pushed harder. Even after the makeover, she felt insecure about her appearance. What was worse was the way her body gravitated toward his. She *yearned* for him. And it was appalling. How could she still want him after everything he'd done to her?

But his voice — his words — had her reacting to him so powerfully.

She disgusted herself.

Jackie ducked under his arm and stalked away as fast as she could.

A wry laugh came from behind her and something that sounded like he'd said, "Just like old times," but she wasn't going to stop and find out what he meant by that.

Not about to go back into the restaurant and answer questions, Jackie pulled out her phone and texted

Caroline to tell her that she was okay and that she was going to hide out in her room for a while.

On the way, she couldn't help but notice the signs for the pool. With no one to miss her, why shouldn't she take advantage of what was sure to be a beautiful and relaxing space?

She dashed back to her room and quickly unlocked the door. Only this time, without the stunned haze of seeing Logan again clouding her vision, she paused to really take in the room. Or perhaps it was the sheer luxury that gave her pause. It proved just how much his presence had rattled her.

She studied the grain of the polished wood underfoot as she strolled through. Somehow the room managed to keep the feel of the island and combine it with the lavishness for which Totally Five Star was renowned.

Jackie's hand was drawn to the wooden headboard to trace the intricate designs. Flowers and vines decorated the indigenous grayish-blue mahoe and while they were wonderfully carved, she could tell each leaf and petal had been lovingly etched by hand. Gossamer curtains hung over the bed and were probably more decorative than functional, but it gave the ambiance a nice touch. What took her breath away were the two enormous windows that served as walls, giving her an incredible view of the ocean and the islands. And the beautiful natural rock surrounding the pool and balcony.

It was so tempting to just conceal herself in her little sanctuary. Hiding away from the world had been her MO for far too long. Here she was in an incredible place and she was thinking of doing just that.

No more.

Besides, she had to make the most of her vacation and sulking in her room was the complete opposite. Away from home and her responsibilities for the first time in recent memory, Jackie wasn't going to waste it.

After changing into her suit then grabbing her things, she held her head high and strode out.

The path to the pool surprised her. Jackie hadn't expected an intricate network of suspended stone sidewalks crisscrossing through the air leading from building to building, from crag to rock face. *Incredible.*

Feeling like Indiana Jones, Jackie slowly walked across. Not because she was scared, but because she had to take in everything. The sights, the sounds, the smells. She wanted to score it all into her memory.

Jackie followed the arrows leading her along a series of paths suspended in the valley between two moss-covered rock faces. She couldn't help hanging over the railing to get a look at the scenery beneath or stopping to try to see how the engineers suspended the stone. When she finally reached the poolside, the sunlight blinded her for a moment. Falling as it was toward the horizon, the sun was still brilliant compared to what had filtered into the shaded spot where she had been.

Blinking until her vision cleared, Jackie took a moment to gaze at the rippling surface of the beautifully clear pool and the sapphire ocean beyond. Lush emerald islands jutted out of the ocean in the distance, breaking up the serene surface. It certainly was a perfect location for a resort. The hotel sat poised on the mountaintop overlooking the water on one side and the rest of the island on the other. It was like being on top of the world.

Jackie might not have been running in the same circles anymore, but she did know that the Totally Five Star chain encompassed some of the most incredible hotels in the world. This one definitely not withstanding.

Inhaling the fresh sea air, she spread her towel on a sun lounger with a deft flick of her wrist. Jackie wasted no time before diving into the crystalline water. Floating weightless in the blissful coolness, she stayed under as long as she could before her lungs burned for air. She kicked up to the surface to float on her back under the glare of the sun. Jackie almost wished she'd brought a skimpier suit so she wouldn't get a tan line as though she'd worn a horse blanket the whole time she was in St. Lucia.

Then again, who would know? She couldn't remember the last time she'd had a date, let alone the last time one had led to sex. Or at least something that could have been loosely defined as sex. It had been so dull and unsatisfying that she hadn't bothered trying again since.

Sex had never been like the mindless, all-consuming passion that she and Logan had shared while they were together. Just being in the same room again brought back all the memories — the feelings — and it was overwhelming, especially after keeping them all tamped down for so long.

He was a bit more muscular, a lot more serious, but he was still Logan Forrester. The one man she had loved more than life itself just as she was coming to grips with herself — with who she was. The man who had turned her life upside down, very nearly ruining it. And yet, she still felt the same stomach-flipping, mind-reeling, knee-knocking attraction to him.

It had to be the memories of what they'd once had influencing her reaction upon seeing him again. Chances were that the memories she had were addled and more than likely exaggerated by the horribly bad sex she'd had over the years.

That had to be it. There was no way sex with anyone could be as good as she imagined it to be.

Jackie could tell herself that as much as she wanted, but she knew she was deluding herself. When he'd had her pinned against the wall, she could feel the chemistry between them simmering. What would it be like if he actually touched her?

She wouldn't let him.

How could she even consider it?

Because as much as she wanted to deny it, he was the most amazing sex she'd ever had and it'd been too long since she'd felt the way she had when she was with him.

Jackie dimly heard a splash, and her body bobbed when the water rippled past her. As much as she would have liked to have the pool to herself, it was open to everyone at the hotel. Perfectly content to just drift, she let herself be propelled by the tiny waves caused by whoever it was that had dove into the water.

A few a more people seemed to be drawn to the water and soaking up sunshine just as she was, not that she could blame them. With the blaring heat of the day waning, a cool dip in the pool was a wonderful way to start the evening. Feminine voices came from the women gathering on the deck not too far away and loungers scraped against stone as they settled onto them on the other side.

Jackie sensed herself getting closer to the glass edge of the infinity pool and righted herself so she could cross her arms over the lip and enjoy the world-class view. As the water lapped over the side, it took the stress from her encounter with Logan with it.

It had been a long time since she'd been somewhere so opulent. It seemed longer still since she'd seen something that encouraged her to just stop and stare. The scenery was breathtaking, from the incredible colors of the water and islands to the exotic scents filling her lungs with every breath.

Jackie made a mental note to find out what else there was to offer in the hotel and outside on the rest of the island. If she had to go exploring on her own and spend a little more than she had, so be it. It wasn't like she was going to get the opportunity again for a long time.

Not that she hated her life. Unless she was around people who regularly associated with her parents or people who wintered elsewhere, Jackie was quite proud of what she had done with what life had dealt her.

She'd finished school. It might not have been what she had originally intended, but becoming a teacher had been rewarding. The children she taught were a pleasure, for the most part. There were a few here and there who tested her patience, but even then, she enjoyed her job. It afforded her a little house and a comfortable life — and her independence.

She wouldn't have traded that for anything.

But when she found herself with people who looked down their noses at '*that* Pennington girl', it put up her defenses and made her want to justify her choices, even though she knew there was no need. There was no logical reason why their opinions should matter to her.

It meant that she spent most of her life avoiding their world. Which, of course, made any time she re-emerged a cause for unrelenting questions and updates on people's lives that she really didn't care or want to hear about.

She'd been prepared to endure it for Caroline. Her friend had been the only one who had bothered to keep in touch.

Someone else dove in behind her, sending more water over the lip, but she didn't expect them to approach her.

"You've got your deep-in-thought face on."

Jackie jumped at his gratingly familiar voice a millisecond before he floated to her side.

She fought her face into a tranquil expression. "I *was* trying to relax."

He turned to study her, throwing his arms over the glass to hold himself in place. "If that's the face you're making, you're relaxing wrong."

She glared at him. "Maybe it's the company."

"Ouch." He still didn't look away.

"If you're not going to leave, then I am." Jackie pushed off the wall, propelling herself through the water. That was until a hand closed around her ankle and dragged her back.

Jackie kicked at him with her free leg, but to no avail.

Logan hauled her up against him as easily as if she were a child. Wrapping his arms around her, he held her in place. "Hush, princess. You don't want to cause a scene, do you?"

"Let me go right now."

"Or you'll what?"

At his challenge, she lifted her chin a notch. "I'll scream the walls down."

"You and I both know that will never happen," Logan scoffed, shifting himself closer. "Not unless I'm doing something else to you."

Their bathing suits might as well not have been there. Jackie felt every inch of him, many of which prodded insistently and ignited panic within her. It shot like a bolt through her, and she shoved at his shoulder, his chest, wherever she could. She found only hard, unyielding, muscle. "Logan, this is inappropriate."

"But that's what makes it so exciting." He leaned closer and growled in her ear. "Isn't that why you went slumming it with me in the first place? The thrill?"

Jackie jerked back to look at him. The difference in their social standings had nothing to do with her attraction to him. It hadn't been even a minor factor. What burned between them had been purely chemical — physical. Though, they did have a lot in common outside of the bedroom as well. She'd thought he knew that.

A dull ache throbbed in the vicinity of her heart. "You're an ass."

His smile grew, and he pressed closer still. "One that you couldn't keep your hands off, if I remember correctly."

"That was a long time ago. Things have changed." Jackie tried to edge away, but the glass wall was even more unyielding than his body. "Will you please give me my space?"

"So simple just to ask, isn't it?" he growled. He glared at her, his eyes dark. "Why couldn't you have done that before?"

Jackie stared at him, confused. "What are you talking about?"

Logan shook his head at her question. "What does it matter now? What's interesting at the moment is how our bodies don't seem to register that we haven't seen each other in years." He ground his solid erection against her — as if she hadn't already noticed.

Conflicted, Jackie wanted to wind herself around him and feel more of Logan's hard body against hers, but she needed to run. "You're disgusting."

"Are you telling me that you're not the least bit interested?" Logan dropped his gaze pointedly to her chest.

Jackie followed it to stare down at herself and the peaks of her nipples straining through the thin fabric of her swimsuit. She crossed her arms protectively. "Don't flatter yourself. It's the cold water."

"So it's the water that makes your breath hitch when I touch you?" He lazily ran his finger delicately over her collarbone and her breath did exactly what he'd said.

"That was the breeze," she grumbled.

"Funny. I didn't feel a thing." He quirked an eyebrow. "Is it the sun that makes your pupils dilate and your skin flush?"

Jackie knew her skin bristled with goosebumps. She'd just hoped he wouldn't notice. Considering how closely Logan was studying her, it was pointless worrying. Of course he did. It didn't stop her from denying her body's response to him. "It certainly isn't you."

Logan shrugged, drawing her gaze to the taut skin and movement of muscle the action caused. He looked good. Disgustingly so.

"I guess it won't matter to you then that I haven't been able to stop thinking about you since I saw you in the lobby."

What could she say? She hadn't been able to focus on anything else either. But she wasn't about to admit it.

"Or if I told you I've been sporting a hard-on for just as long?"

That was definitely something she didn't need to hear. "Logan, will you stop?"

"Not until you admit you want me as much as I want you."

"At which you'll turn around and suggest that since we still want each other we might as well take advantage of it."

He grinned broadly. "So you *do* still want me."

"I never said that."

"You don't think I can tell?" He smirked. "I know you, Jackie. I know your body. You might as well be waving me in."

Jaw slack, she shook her head at him. "Still the sweet-talker."

Logan leaned in close so she could feel the warmth of his breath on her cheek and neck.

His husky voice, he said, "As I recall, you didn't like sweet."

Jackie bristled, even though she knew he spoke the truth. She hadn't wanted hearts and flowers. All she'd wanted was Logan. Any way and anywhere she could get him.

She had made it almost embarrassingly easy for him. "Turn around."

He'd lowered his voice to a pitch that reminded her of what he sounded like during sex. Afterward. And he knew it.

Jackie didn't move a muscle. Mostly because she was preoccupied with memories of when he'd used that voice on her in the past.

When she continued to stare at him, Logan closed his hands around her hips and slowly spun her around until she looked upon the undulating ocean again.

"What are you doing?" Jackie tried to turn back but he held her in place against the glass with the weight of his body. Excitement spiked, even as apprehension wormed its way into the back of her mind. "Logan."

"Shh." He notched the wide ridge of his erection into the cleft of her ass.

Jackie fought the urge to press back against him. It was completely insane. She should hate him. But inexplicably, stupidly, she wanted him. The ache felt worryingly close to need. The same response that used to cloud all her judgment took over her consciousness until there was nothing but Logan.

He slid his large hand up her side to cup her breast.

Jackie gripped the lip of the wall. "Stop. Someone is going to see."

He pressed his cheek to hers. "Not if you don't make a scene."

It wasn't easy, especially when he curved his other hand around her hip and traced the edge of her swimsuit with his fingers. Heat flared. Every stroke sent shafts of sensation to a place deep behind her belly button.

Jackie knew that it was just the tip of the iceberg. The sensations the man could evoke... Did she dare lose herself in them again?

It was so tempting. Why shouldn't she have a little fun? And why not use the man who had been the cause of the dramatic changes in her life? At least she knew she'd get satisfaction out of being with him. Use him and toss him, just like he'd done to her. Meanwhile, having some fantastic sex would distract her from having to deal with the gawkers and leave her with good memories to last her.

Decision made, she shifted, sliding that tiny bit so his fingers slipped just under her suit.

Jackie felt his smile against her cheek, heard it in his voice.

"That's my girl." Logan eased his finger inside and twisted his hand back and forth to slide another in with it. "Still so tight."

"Will you shut up?" Jackie didn't want anyone catching on to their game and stopping them.

"As you wish, princess." His voice had lowered, taken on a husky, gravelly quality he knew she loved. Logan rocked his hand, slowly pumping his fingers in and out. He knew exactly what to do, the pressure, the rhythm, to surely build her toward a searing orgasm.

Jackie's breath began to hitch as he quickened the pace. Her fingers and toes tingled. Her muscles slowly contracted as she got closer to climax.

Grazing her clit with the heel of his hand, he slowed his movements. It earned him a disappointed mewl from Jackie.

She arched against him, seeking his hand, needing more friction.

"What's the matter, princess? Am I not pleasing you?"

"Logan." Jackie fought to keep the whine out of her voice, but from his chuckle, she assumed she'd failed.

"Ask nicely." He nipped her earlobe as he waited. Sucked it.

She wriggled and repeated his name.

Logan sighed, plunging his fingers deeper before sliding them almost all the way out.

Jackie growled at him, but refused to plead.

He huffed a humor-filled breath, but said nothing as he twisted his fingers and thumbed her clit in gentle circles. It was good. But it wasn't enough to bring her what she wanted. Jackie writhed against him, trying her best to find some satisfaction.

"Still as stubborn as ever, I see." The friction turned into a slippery, less satisfying slide of his fingers.

Pinned as she was, she couldn't get any leverage. Couldn't get the friction that she wanted—needed. She was just so close. If he would just add a little pressure. Do that thing with his fingers that had always sent her over the edge. "Please, Logan."

"That's right, princess. You know who does it for you."

Logan rubbed the ridge of his cock into the cleft of her ass as he plunged his fingers inside her again, hitting all the right places to build her up into a spectacular orgasm.

Her entire being converged to a single pinpoint then exploded.

Logan smothered her cries with his free hand while wringing out the rest of her orgasm.

Jackie sagged against the wall dazedly trying to catch her breath. As she came down from the high, Jackie realized what she had let him do. What she had begged him to do. In broad daylight. In clear view of everyone in the pool area.

What the hell had she been thinking?

Thinking? That was the problem. Whenever she was around Logan, her brain took a back seat. So, while she had an amazing time with him, it wasn't good enough. At least, it hadn't been enough to keep them together.

Euphoria burned away to be replaced by mortification in an instant. Jackie wriggled free. Shame kept her eyes on the water as she darted past him to swim away.

He closed a gentle hand around her wrist, stopping her. "Hey."

"I've got to go."

He hauled her against him. "You don't."

She allowed him to hold her, but glared at him. "I don't know what game you're playing, Logan, but I can't do this."

Not again.

Logan held her stiff body against his and stared down into the face that featured in his dreams far too often for his liking. He hated that she was still so attractive to him. That he still wanted her with a burning ferocity that made no sense.

What had started out as a game, a test to see if she was still as responsive to him as he remembered, had turned into something more. Something infinitely more dangerous.

He couldn't afford to lose himself in Jackie again. Logan knew she had the ability to make him forget about everything. What they'd shared blotted all else out until there was nothing but the two of them. At least that's how it had been for him.

Jackie had once been the center of his world.

Never again.

That didn't exclude some time together this week, though. It would be a means of getting closure. She'd just proved that she still responded to him as if there had been no time lost between them. Jackie had reacted so readily and come so quickly and sweetly around his fingers that it had almost pushed him over the edge with her.

And now he wanted to see if she still responded to him in other ways.

Though, considering how she ran away from him, that would be a harder sell.

Hard. Not impossible.

As he recalled, persuading her could be a lot of fun. Once he got past her barriers… His groin throbbed at the images that flashed through his mind. Then he could get her out of his system and get on with his life. He just had to convince her to let him in.

"Jackie. Think about it. What are the odds of us meeting up again? In a place like this?"

She narrowed her eyes at him in condemnation. "Next you'll tell me it's kismet. That the cosmos wants us to be together."

"And if it does?"

Jackie shoved at his shoulders. "You were never a sap. Stop bullshitting me."

There was the fire he was looking for.

He smirked. "I'll tell you what isn't BS." Logan stared her straight in the eyes. "This thing between us. The chemistry is still there. Don't say you can't feel it because I know you can." He tipped her chin up with his finger to look at him before settling his hands on her shoulders. "We've got a five-star hotel at our disposal for a week. I'm thinking we could make the most of our time here."

"Then we simply part ways? How convenient." She brushed his hands off her. "I'm not interested."

Logan smirked. "Liar."

"I'm not lying," she snarled.

"Prove it." Logan leaned in close enough to smell her. "Kiss me."

Shit.

Spending time with Logan didn't sound bad. As much as she hated to admit it, she wanted more of what she knew he could give her. But she refused to say it to his face.

And now he wanted her to kiss him to prove she wasn't interested? There was no way she could do that without making her attraction to him incredibly obvious. As if she hadn't already proven he had her wrapped around his little finger.

Just the thought of his fingers sent a tremor through her. After what he'd just done, it was quite apparent what he could do to her with the rest of his body. Would it be so bad to enjoy that—enjoy him—again? She was smart and mature enough now to handle him.

Wasn't she?

There was one way to prove it to herself and him.

Jackie tunneled her hands through his hair and dragged his head down. There was a brief look of surprise on his face before their mouths met somewhere in the middle.

The sexy groan he uttered sparked heat low in her belly, as if he hadn't just given her a toe-curling orgasm.

She might have been the one to instigate, but Logan took full control. He parted her lips expertly and tasted her with teasing strokes. Jackie clung to him, the sensation of his mouth against her bringing back a myriad of memories and evoking so many more at the same time. The tumultuous mix left her weak in the knees.

Logan flicked her bottom lip with his tongue as he drew back, keeping her pressed tightly against him. "I'm taking it that you're not opposed to my proposition."

Definitely not. "Not as such, but we need to lay down some rules."

"As I recall, we never needed rules before."

She edged back a little. "Well, I think we do now. The situation is a little different, isn't it?"

His eyes darkened. "It is." Logan studied her a moment, stared into her eyes. "So? What kinds of rules do you have in mind?"

Jackie pursed her lips. It wasn't something she knew much about. What did she know about casual sex? "I guess we should start with the basics."

Logan smiled as he crept his hands around to cup her ass. "Basics, huh?"

The feel of his big hands on her ruined the arguments she could barely formulate in the first place. What was she thinking? Basics? "Yeah," she croaked. "Like…"

"Like…?" he urged. Logan lowered one of his hands, sweeping it over her thigh.

Jackie swatted at his hand. "Will you stop that?"

"Sorry." Only his smile proved that he wasn't. "Should we make the rules up as we go…?"

And let him change them as they went along? Hell no! "Why don't we get out of the pool and go get a drink so we can hash this out?"

"Whatever you like, princess."

"Stop calling me that."

Chapter Four

She might have gotten out of the pool, but Jackie hadn't taken into account the fact that she would then have to walk with him, mostly naked and without the protection of other hotel patrons. She pulled the towel tighter around her shoulders, careful to hide as much of her skin as possible.

Meanwhile, the man next to her seemed perfectly at ease sauntering alongside her in nothing but his shorts.

She wouldn't look at him. She wouldn't.

Despite her best intentions, Jackie couldn't help herself. Logan certainly hadn't gotten any less handsome. Watching the droplets of water slowly skate over his muscles was only slightly more distracting than seeing the few sparkling in his sparse chest hair. She tried tearing her eyes away, but as they turned the corner, the waning sunlight hit the water just right and Jackie couldn't help but watch it lazily find a path down his pecs, over his rippling abs and into the waistband of his shorts.

Jackie gulped, startling herself. He must have heard it. A quick look had her breathing easy. Logan was more interested in the scenery than what she was doing.

She brushed her hair out of her face. "Okay, I'm going to get changed. I'll meet you at the bar in ten minutes."

He paused to look her over. "Sure you don't want me to go with you?"

Logan's smile was far too appealing. It was too soon. She needed to set some rules before letting him come anywhere near her bed.

"I'll be quick."

He smirked. "As I recall, it took you at least forty-five minutes to get ready for anything."

She rolled her eyes at him. "Like I keep saying, things have changed. Ten minutes. At the bar."

He nodded with a small smile. "See you there."

Jackie hurried to her room. She wasn't about to waste any time after making a point about how much she'd changed. It was the truth, however. With fewer clothes to choose from, less time and not as many snooty opinions to worry about, getting dressed was a breeze.

Though now she had Logan's judgment to deal with.

She dragged her tiny suitcase to the bed and quickly rooted through it, looking for anything that would be sexy but casual.

Jackie had a total of one dress that fit the bill. It was classy and revealed just enough skin to even be described as sexy, but she was saving it for at least one dinner during the week. Maybe two if she disguised it with a wrap or perhaps a jacket.

She grabbed a pair of jeans and a T-shirt. They would have to do.

After a quick shower, light makeup, putting her hair up in a ponytail and sliding into sandals, the outfit looked cute and casual. Good enough for a non-date at the hotel bar.

Only Jackie had underestimated the type of bar she was to walk into. The moment she strolled in the door she knew she'd miscalculated. The rest of the patrons looked like something out of a vacation brochure for the rich and famous. Men wore jackets for the most part. The ones who didn't wore button-downs and pressed trousers. The women might as well have been gracing a catwalk.

And there she was in ratty old jeans and a faded T-shirt.

Why had she imagined a Totally Five Star Hotel bar filled with tiki torches and kitschy décor?

Because I don't belong in this world anymore.

On the verge of turning on her heel and dashing back to her room to change into the dress, she heard Logan's familiar drawl.

"Jackie. Right on time." He smiled broadly as he sauntered over. Like her, he wore jeans and a T-shirt, but he didn't seem to give a damn that he stood out like a handsome sore thumb.

Logan curved his arm around her waist to steer her to the drinks he had waiting at the bar. He picked them up, but before handing one over to her he asked, "Want to go outside?"

Nodding, she led the way. Anything to get away from the censure clear in the looks she was receiving from all around.

She walked straight out onto the balcony where others had had the same idea. Logan took the lead then, using his big body to plow a path through the crowd. He finally led them to the wide railing and set the drinks down on it.

The view took Jackie's breath away. The incredible splashes of purple, red and gold fought for dominance overhead and into the horizon.

"Gorgeous, isn't it?"

"It is." Jackie absentmindedly picked up her drink and delicately tasted it. Once the flavors came together on her tongue she smiled. "You remembered."

Chuckling, he took a slug of his beer.

She copied him, tipping the glass back further for more. "So, why are you here? Did Charles talk you into it?"

Logan shook his head. "I'm actually here to work."

"Yeah? What do you do now?"

"I handle the security systems here and in all the Totally Five Star Hotels."

Jackie grinned at him. "I knew you'd make it."

The easy smile faded from his face. "Did you?"

The air between them crackled, but it wasn't sexual tension. The shift in mood had her rocking from foot to foot. "Why don't we keep the past out of this? And the future too, for that matter."

"Fine by me."

The old hurt throbbed in her chest at his dismissive tone. If he could make her hurt with just a few words in one conversation, what could he do to her after a week? "You know what? This was a bad idea." Jackie pushed the glass away. "Thanks for the drink. I'll see you at the rehearsals." For the dinner, the wedding, then the event itself. She would have to see him at each one. There would be no avoiding him.

She made it to the door before his hand closed around her wrist.

"Jackie." Logan held tightly when she tried to pull her arm from his grasp. "Dance with me."

"Have you completely lost it?" Jackie whipped her arm away from him.

Logan snared her hand and dragged her close. "Just shut up and dance."

The way Jackie scrambled his brain pissed him off, but he couldn't let her get away. From the instant she walked into the bar looking so cute and perfect, he knew he was in over his head. And he hadn't been the only one to notice her. Logan fought away the very visceral need to take out every man staring at her.

On the balcony, she stared at the horizon, as if she'd never seen anything so beautiful. He probably had the same expression on his face as he stared at her.

Jackie was still the most breathtaking woman he'd ever seen. When she'd threatened to leave, he'd done the only thing that came to mind. One of the best times they'd ever had, while clothed, was when they'd danced on a beach. Well, they were at the beach now and they couldn't get naked. Yet. But he would work on it.

The way she'd responded to him in the pool was proof that she still wanted him, and he would use that to his advantage. Not that he doubted the chemistry between them. It was potent and almost palpable. Even if they weren't going to admit it, they were undeniably attracted to each other.

Even now, with her anger and reticence coming off her in waves, he had only to look into her eyes to see that she felt the same attraction he did.

Logan pulled her against him, and they fell into time with the soft beat of the music. His body reacted immediately at the feel of her body pressed to his, further proving his theory. He needed to work off this tension.

"You're right. This is a terrible idea, but I can't just let you walk away. Not after meeting again after all this time. It might not be kismet or fate, but we're here, so I'm just suggesting we make the most of it." Logan have her a hint of a smile. "Your rule is also good. We should just keep this about here and now. What happened, happened. Nothing we can do to change that now."

He caught the glint of tears in her eyes. Did she regret what had happened between them? Jackie kept her eyes down and her focus on his chest as she nodded.

"Yeah."

"Are you okay?" He tipped her chin so he could look at her, but the tears were gone. He knew he hadn't imagined them. Jackie must have gotten better at controlling her emotions.

She turned her clear gaze up at him. "I'm fine. But yeah, I agree. Here and now. Just us. Nothing else."

Logan's entire body tightened at her words. That was how it had been for him their entire time together. How it had never been with anyone else. Only it hadn't been enough for her.

This time around, he would make sure that *she* was the one hooked then he would discard her the same way she had him.

Logan rocked them in time with the music, pressing her against him with one arm. The feel of her body against his brought back a tsunami of memories to blend with the sensations that touching her evoked. They'd had some good times together and not only when it came to sex.

He recalled occasions spent just the two of them spread out on a blanket, stargazing on the beach. They were, by far, some of the best memories he'd had, and it hadn't cost a dime.

Things had changed for him since. Money was no longer a problem. He didn't have to think twice about anything anymore. There was no more penny pinching. If he wanted something, he bought it. If there was a place he wanted to go, he could be there the next morning. Nothing was out of the realm of possibility any longer. He had everything he could possibly, except for one thing. Logan had kept himself largely solitary since Jackie. There were women here and there, but there hadn't been anyone who'd tempted him to settle down.

Never again had become his mantra.

That, however, didn't exclude a few one-night stands. As hot as they were, every single one of them was eclipsed by the mere memory of Jackie.

And now he had the chance to experience it all again. His dick throbbed at the thought. After that little interlude in the pool, he was more than ready. And she was too. At least she was physically.

He just had to get her mind in synch with her body.

What fun that would be.

She tried to focus her attention anywhere but him, but failed miserably. After so long apart, Jackie kept finding bits of him to compare with his old self. What had changed. What hadn't. To her consternation, she could pick out every minute difference.

Why was she able to do it? Why did she even care?

Jackie stared at the lights in the ceiling in an attempt to distract herself. So pretty. They actually looked like stars. Just over their heads was a cluster that almost looked like the Big Dipper constellation.

Someone bumped her just as they turned, sending her toppling into Logan. Without pause, he gripped her to him and kept her steady with one arm while he cocked the other back aggressively. For an agonizingly long moment, she thought he was going to punch the other guy out.

The man, who looked more suited to a fight in the boardroom than in a bar, put up his hands in apology and hurried away.

She glared at Logan. Even though her heart had picked up its pace, she was far from hurt. What he'd done had been a gross overreaction. One that had drawn far too much attention. She dragged his arm back down to his side. "You can't go beating people up over me, you know. Not anymore."

It took him a long while to draw his attention away from the man to focus on her. "I wouldn't let anyone hurt you. Still won't. What kind of man could?"

Jackie wanted to point out the irony of his words. Out of all the hurt she'd endured, did he have any idea that he was the one who had devastated her the most? She almost smiled at the thought of Logan beating himself up.

"I'm serious."

"I can take care of myself." She pushed on his chest and took a big step backward. "And right now, I'm going to go and try to get a good night's sleep." Not likely, but tossing and turning until dawn was preferable to staring at him any longer.

"I'll walk you."

Jackie stopped, turned then stared up at him. "What kind of game are you playing?"

"I'm not." He tried to put his hands on her shoulders, but she kept out of reach, so he let them drop to his sides. "I'm sorry, all right? Seeing you again is bringing back a lot of stuff. I just want a chance to spend some time with you. Get to know you again."

Hadn't they just been discussing rules for a casual sexcapade? "That's not part of the deal."

"Fine. My dick needs to be inside you again. How's that for honest?"

Heat blasted her cheeks at his blunt words. A quick glance around proved that no one had overheard him, thanks to the music.

He edged closer, growling, "I want to bend you over and fuck you until you're a screaming, trembling, sticky mess."

And damned if she didn't want him to.

Slack-jawed, Jackie stared at him for a moment as his words and the images they conjured washed over her. They alone were enough to put a tremble in her knees and slick her panties.

Mind made up, she took his hand and led the way out of the bar.

She turned toward the same path she'd taken on the way over, but Logan tugged her back.

"Over here."

He led her down another trail toward what looked like the mountain. "I've got a faster way."

Jackie hurried to keep up with his long strides, aware of him retrieving his phone and typing something with his free hand. Luckily for him, his hand was big enough to do it easily. She'd never be able to do that and hold onto the device at the same time.

He quickly finished whatever he was doing and pushed her into an elevator. Jackie hadn't even known it existed. Then again, she hadn't had much opportunity to explore since she'd arrived.

They entered and he pressed the button to close the door before anyone else could follow. He jammed his thumb against the number for the top floor before spinning around and gathering her up in his arms once again. Pushing her back against the wooden wall, Logan grinned before he went to work on the fastening of her jeans.

Jackie gripped his shoulders, seeking his mouth with hers, only dimly aware of anything other than Logan. He shoved her jeans down her legs, trapping her feet. With a parting nip at her bottom lip, he slid down to his knees. Logan closed his hands around her hips and dipped his tongue between her thighs.

Holding back a squeal, Jackie spread her legs as much as she could and remain upright.

Logan took full advantage of the better access. Kissing her folds, he parted them with his fingers and immediately slipped his tongue into her, humming appreciatively as he did so.

He licked and sucked, murmuring as if he'd never tasted anything so good and wanted as much as he could get. He added his fingers, quickly multiplying the heady sensations clouding her mind, winding her body tighter.

It was madness. Pure lust coursed through her veins, blocking out everything but the pleasure only Logan seemed to be able to draw out of her.

Jackie let her head fall back as her orgasm slammed into her. Reeling, she clung to him for several breathless moments as she tried to regain her balance—her control. What was it about him that always had her throwing caution to the wind?

It had been good—more than—but they were in a damned elevator for goodness' sake. She craned her neck to find the cameras she knew would be there.

Cringing, she pushed herself off the wall. "Logan... The cameras."

"Don't worry about it." He gripped the waist of her jeans and pulled them up. "What we do need to concern ourselves with is that we're almost at our floor."

Her movements were jerky with panic, but she helped him tug her jeans back in place and had rebuttoned them seconds before the doors slid open.

Ignoring the knowing glances of the people waiting to get on, he swept them past as calm and collected as ever. At least to anyone who didn't know him. Jackie could see the glow in his eyes and the set of his jaw. Logan was barely hanging on to his control.

The revelation made her smile a little. At least she wasn't the only one affected by the chemistry between them.

He led the way, striding ahead with a clear destination in mind.

It wasn't long before they were charging across another path toward a building on its own, perched high above all the others.

Swiping a card over the reader, he pushed the door open the instant there was a muted beep.

Logan turned to her then, held her gaze. Was he giving her a chance to back out? Was this what she really wanted? It took her a split second to come to her conclusion. They didn't need words. She tightened her grip on his hand.

He sighed—was that relief?—before Logan picked her up and kicked the door closed behind them.

Chapter Five

Logan gently put her down, whipped Jackie's T-shirt up and off then threw it behind him. He stared down at her, her torso bare except for the thin lace bra holding her small breasts. Logan had once convinced her to stop wearing them. It wasn't like she needed the support. He had loved seeing how easily he could arouse her nipples to hard little peaks. Or just being able to slip his hands up under her clothes and graze her creamy, bare skin.

It had served as a test on him at the time as well. Pushing himself to his limits of self-control. Not that it would take much to push him over the edge when it came to Jackie. All she had to do was look at him, smile, flutter her lashes, bite her lip — breathe in his general direction — and he would get hard. Then chances were they'd find a quiet niche somewhere and they'd temporarily burn out the tension. His body was, and very obviously always would be, ready for her.

"This is coming off." He quickly disposed of the bra. He needed to see her bare. With it gone, he took a moment to just stare. Her pale skin was as smooth as he remembered. Her nipples the same dusky pink that reminded him of the sky just as the sun set during the summer.

God, she was beautiful.

The sight of them made his mouth water.

Tasting her in the elevator had been heaven. There had been times when he'd dreamed about spreading her under him and feasting on her as he had just moments before and he'd woken, craving her. Or, out of nowhere, he would experience something as simple as hearing a song and knew she would enjoy it and wished he could share it with her.

It annoyed him.

It saddened him.

Frustrated the shit out of him.

He shook off the melancholy. He was with her now. Again. He would make the most of it.

Impatient, Logan flicked the button of her jeans through the loop and yanked the zipper before tugging them down her legs, taking her panties with them.

Jackie kicked them off and stood before him, her eyes averted almost as if she was…ashamed?

"Hey, what's the matter?" He tipped her chin up so her gaze met his.

She shook her head. "Nothing. I just need you naked."

Her statement shot straight to his groin, but he pushed her hands away when she reached for his shirt. "Are you regretting this?"

Jackie's eyes widened slightly. "No."

"Then what is it?"

"I… I'm not the same." She huffed a breath when he just stared at her, waiting for an explanation. "I'm not the skinny girl I used to be, all right? It bothers me."

It took a long moment for her words to sink in. She was worried about how she looked? There was nothing wrong that he could see. Jackie might not be as waifish as she had been, but she was hardly obese. Far from it.

Logan gripped her hand and pressed it to his erection. "Does it feel like it bothers me?"

She didn't look amused, though she curved her hand to cup him for an instant before pulling away. "You're staring at a naked woman, Logan. Of course you're hard."

He swore under his breath. Where had the self-confident woman he'd known gone? "If you think I get this hard for just any naked woman, you're wrong. If you honestly believe I'd just go down on any random woman in an elevator, you're out of your mind."

Logan ran his hands down her arms to slide them up over her hips and waist before bringing them to a stop to cup her breasts. "I've been going out of my mind trying to keep my body under control ever since I saw you in the lobby. Whatever it is between us hasn't burned out and it isn't anything I've experienced with anyone else."

The look in her eyes morphed into something else. The reticence had given way to something a little bit like awe and a lot like desire.

She licked her lips, sucking in the bottom one to nibble on pensively as she considered his words.

Logan tugged his shirt off and quickly shucked his jeans to stand bare before her. Her eyes widened as she let her gaze rove over him. Her breath picked up pace and her skin flushed as she stared. Jackie obviously still found his body a turn-on if her reaction was anything to go by.

He waved his hand over himself. "I've changed a lot too. You don't see me worrying about it."

The expression on her face shuttered a little. "That's because you look fantastic."

"And so do you."

Jackie didn't get a chance to respond. Logan picked her up and wound her legs around his hips as he dropped his head to capture her mouth with his. Carrying her over to the curtain-shrouded bed, he then placed her on it and followed close behind.

If she had any concerns that he found any part of her unattractive, they were soon blown away. Logan gazed at her as if she was the most beautiful woman he had ever seen. He worshiped all the parts of her that he could reach, as if he couldn't get enough.

He caressed her. Kissed her. It seemed as though he needed her more than air.

Jackie clung to him. The last time she had kissed anyone and felt the same way — the same urgency and fire — was the last time she'd kissed Logan before he had disappeared.

The memory sent a shaft of hurt lancing through her. She didn't want to think about that. Jackie wanted to feel what only Logan was capable of doing to her.

He cupped her cheeks as he gave her another biting kiss. Ran his hands over her skin as though he was trying to memorize the feel. Or perhaps compare the reality of her now to the girl in his memories.

He followed the path his hands blazed with his mouth, tracing with his lips — his tongue — nipping gently as he went.

Jackie arched, needing more contact, wanting to feel more of Logan. Clawing her nails into his back, she attempted to drag him closer, but other than a slight hiss, he didn't seem to notice. He seemed intent on exploring her at his leisure.

He slowly kissed and licked his way down her body. Logan paid lavish attention to her breasts. He teased them with his hands, tweaking her nipples between his finger and thumb before sucking one into his hot mouth. The sensation of him drawing on her sensitive flesh, him laving her with his tongue, was exquisite. It curled her toes and brought a sigh to her lips.

It quickly turned into a keening cry when he brought his hands back into play.

Logan hooked his arms around her thighs and gripped them as he wedged his torso between.

With a wicked grin, he lowered his head and ran his tongue along her slick folds. Logan groaned his appreciation before pressing his tongue deeper, delving into her. He lapped at her slowly, curling his tongue to great effect.

Jackie closed her eyes, not wanting anything to interfere with her experiencing the zaps of pleasure pin-balling through her with each glancing touch of his tongue.

But it was when he closed his lips over her clit that a screaming orgasm raced through her, convulsing her under him, bucking her against his mouth.

Logan gentled his touch, but continued to lick and suck until she sagged under him and clutched at his head, trying to pull him away from her over-sensitized flesh.

He lifted his head and gave her a small smile before he lowered it again.

There was no way she could take any more just then. Jackie squirmed out from under him then pushed on his shoulders until he let her topple him to his side. She let her hands roam over his taut skin, admiring how solid he was and the intriguing play of light and shadows.

He was beautiful.

"You're staring."

She shrugged. There was no point in denying it. He was definitely worth a good ogling. "You want me to stop?"

He shook his head. "There are other things I want you to do."

She closed her hand around his erection, squeezing gently as she slid it up and down over him. Could a man get any bigger? Because she was sure he had since she'd touched him last.

"Something wrong?"

"Not at all." Jackie let her eyes follow the muscles of his arms up to his shoulders and across his chest before meeting his gaze

Logan ran his hands over her waist to bump over her hips and back up again as she continued to pump him.

"You feel incredible."

Jackie chuckled. "So do you."

She lowered her other hand to cup his balls and continued to stroke him. A shudder rippled through him as he groaned.

Confidence surged through her, prompting her to make her way down his body, licking and kissing a path until she was face to face with his magnificent cock.

It was as beautiful and as well formed as the rest of him. Thick and strong, it rose from a dark thatch of hair to the hollow of his belly button. The sight of her hand sliding up and down, unable to close fully around his girth, sent a thrill down her spine. Jackie slid it from root to wide head over and over enjoying the way the tension built in him with each stroke.

Meanwhile, Logan tunneled his hands into her hair, coaxing her closer to him. Clearly, he wanted the same thing she did.

Jackie needed to taste him.

She angled him to her mouth, keeping her gaze on his the entire time. Logan's eyes darkened while he watched her lick the salty bead of pre-cum off the top of his cock. Jackie ran her tongue over the head twice more before taking him into her mouth.

Logan groaned, his hands closed in her hair, tugging her closer, pushing her farther over him as he thrust shallowly into her mouth.

On the next surge, she sucked him deeply, bringing forth a groan and a shudder from Logan.

Jackie bobbed her head and pumped her hand over him, easily remembering the rhythm—the pressure— that he liked. That drove him wild.

A tremor rippled through him. As she continued, it turned into a shudder and a groan. He gripped her hair tighter, almost to the point of pain as Logan thrust into her mouth.

"God, Jackie. So good… I'm going to…"

And he exploded into her mouth, flooding it. As fast as she could swallow, he filled it, until he eventually sagged against her.

Logan slowly slid himself from her mouth as he regained his breath. "That was…"

She knew what he meant. It was the same for her.

"Come on." He held his hand out and got to his feet.

"Where to?" Jackie took it, and he helped her up and swept her into his arms.

He didn't answer, just walked over to the bathroom. Not a word was spoken as he gently set her down and tenderly cleaned her up then himself. Logan then picked her up, taking her back to the bed then lowered her onto it before slipping in beside her.

The sheets were cool in contrast to his hot skin as Logan wound himself around her from behind. It was a position Jackie had loved to be in with Logan. It made her feel so safe and protected. Like he was her shield from the world.

She'd just close her eyes for a moment to enjoy the sensation…

* * * *

When Jackie woke, the moon still shone in the sky. It gave the suite a silvery sheen that simply added to the magnificence of the room.

For a long while, she stared at the way the light played off the net curtains surrounding the bed as they fluttered and danced in the slight breeze. Besides the languid relaxation that left her unwilling to move, there was a cold ball of dread growing in her gut. What was she doing? Sure, Logan had given her some superb orgasms — ones that she had wanted — but waking up in bed with him was another thing altogether. It was too familiar. Brought back too many memories.

It set a dangerous precedent.

She took a moment to study the man next to her. In sleep, Logan's features had softened somewhat. Jackie ran her finger over the furrow in his brow. That was new. While they were together it had been easy to make him smile. It had been nice to be with someone who truly seemed to take joy in life. That wasn't to say he wasn't driven. She had never seen anyone work so hard to achieve his goals. Especially when compared to the rich boys she knew were only at school because they saw it as a constant party before they claimed their rightful place in their families' businesses.

She admired Logan for it. He hadn't taken anything for granted. Hadn't had a thing given to him. Yet she had known Logan would go further than anyone else she knew.

And she had been right, if this suite was any indication.

Jackie slipped out of the massive and immensely comfortable bed to walk toward the huge panes of glass that served as windows and walls. The natural wood was warm beneath her bare feet. Jackie could feel small variations in the grain as she padded her way across. At the window, she ran her fingers along the cold glass as she made her way to the one that had been left open, allowing the exotic scents and cool breeze to enter.

It also cleared a path to his own pool. It was almost bigger and more splendid than the one they had been in outside. Of course it was.

The lights below the water lit it up like a magical grotto beckoning her to dive in. Jackie ignored the urge, preferring to turn her attention to the rest of the room.

The suite was set in an almost circular layout. One side sat nestled into the mountain while the other, the side with the pool on, looked out over the ocean. She could almost imagine the construct appearing like a partially opened clam shell situated on the mountainside. They were quite high—about as high as they could build on the summit. Surely this was a suite saved for esteemed guests and the truly wealthy.

Her gaze went back to the bed to find Logan awake and watching her.

"Did I wake you?"

Shaking his head, Logan threw the blanket back and got up, perfectly at ease with his nudity while at the same time reminding her that she was in a similar state.

She had already started searching the room for her clothes when he reached her.

"Don't you dare." He wound his arms around her from behind and steered her back toward the window.

Jackie tensed, but after a moment of having him cocooning her and the stillness of the night, she eased into his embrace. There was no one to see them and it was wonderful to be skin to skin with Logan. They were in a tropical paradise. Why shouldn't she enjoy herself? If only this was how it could always be.

He rested his chin on her head. "What are you thinking?"

"I feel calmer than I have in a long time. More relaxed."

For a moment, she feared he was going to ask why, but he obviously remembered their rules. No particulars about their lives outside the here and now.

"I'm glad." He tightened his arms, pulling her against his hard chest and his hardening erection.

Jackie turned in his arms to look up at him. "Want to go for a dip in that pool?"

"Absolutely."

He took her hand and led the way. The warmth of the wooden floor gave way to cool rough stone. Instead of stairs, a sandy slope on one side served as the access point to the pool.

They waded in until the bottom gave way and they floated together in harmonious silence.

A further sense of serenity soaked into her with the coolness of the water. She kicked gently to float on her back. It was so freeing that she couldn't keep the small smile from her face. There were no timetables, no prying eyes. Just her, Logan and the night.

They could have been a couple of young adults again. Just hanging out without any demands on their time, no responsibilities. She drifted blissfully for a while before Logan burst up through the water near her head.

He swept her face with his observant gaze. "You look like a weight's been lifted."

Was it that obvious? "How can you not relax in a place like this?"

He pulled her upright. "And here I was thinking that it might have something to do with me."

She smiled at him and replied with a teasing, "Maybe a little." He definitely had something to do with how good she was feeling. He had to know.

Logan gave her a knowing smirk before lowering his head for a kiss that threatened to turn the liquid surrounding them into steam. They sank beneath the surface for a moment before Logan pushed off from the bottom and propelled them to the wall.

The light played off Logan's breathtaking body, rippling and highlighting the droplets running down his handsome face. She followed the path of one with her tongue from his chin and down to his collarbone where she caught up with it and licked it off with a flick of her tongue.

Logan let his eyes drift close as he groaned his appreciation. Another groan rumbled through him as she ran her hands over his hard chest.

He was so incredibly solid, as he had been before, but now there was much more of him to explore. New angles and ridges that invited her fingers to touch and feel.

Not that he had a problem with any of what she was doing to him. In fact, she found a very good indication that he loved it. As much as she hated to admit it, they went well together. At least as far as sex went. There was no denying their compatibility in that department.

He ground himself against her when she curved her hands around his ass and raked her nails over his skin lightly.

"Enjoying yourself, are you?"

"I'd be enjoying it more if you'd stop teasing me," she huffed.

He slid himself over her again, letting her feel every vein in his erection. "What do you want?"

"More of you." All of him.

Logan groaned when she grazed his cock with the back of her hand. "We need to get back in the room for a condom."

Smiling up at him impishly, she closed her hand around him, wanting to tease him.

He took it for a few moments, his body tensing with each passing second, each caress. But when she squeezed him, he carefully pulled her hand away.

"You're evil." He swung her up in his arms and carried her into the room.

She blinked at him innocently. "Silly me. I won't do that ever again."

He lowered her to the bed and crawled over her. "I never said that I wanted you to stop."

Jackie nibbled his bottom lip. "Anything else you don't want me to not stop doing?"

Logan's smile turned wolfish as he retrieved a condom and put it on. "Don't stop smiling?" He pressed the head of his cock against her slit. "Don't stop coming for me?"

Slowly he pushed himself into her, stretching her to the limit.

The likelihood of her not coming while being with him was ludicrous. Logan barely had to touch her before her body hummed with awareness.

Logan slowly shifted himself inside her. Every ridge of his cock rippled past her sensitive skin as he withdrew. He plunged back into her, hitting a delicious spot deep inside before drawing out again, torturously slowly.

The combination scrambled Jackie's mind. With each pump of his hips, her pleasure spiraled higher, her breath coming in gasps each time.

Jackie met each thrust needing more, but the sensations swamped her too quickly.

Logan held her gaze and just as she was about to explode, he ground himself against her clit, enjoying the depth he achieved with the move as much as she did.

She dug her nails into his shoulders as she tried to slow her climb toward climax. She was *there* when he pulled out and flipped her over.

Jackie's cries were muffled by the blankets as he hitched her hips up and slammed back into her. The new angle changed where his strokes reached, but did nothing to dampen the intensity of the sensations exploding in her.

Just when she thought she couldn't take it any longer, he reached around her hip and fingered her clit with a sure hand.

Her world exploded.

Jackie screamed into the bed as he pummeled her. Even through the post-orgasmic haze, she felt his cock getting bigger, harder as his thrusts grew more forceful and his breath hitched.

He slammed into her with a shout. Jackie's orgasm renewed in force at the feel of him pulsing deep inside her.

Logan sagged against her before he tipped them both onto their sides, still lodged firmly inside her.

Still quaking from her orgasm, Jackie sighed happily.

Logan wrapped himself around her again, only drawing back with a grumble to deal with the condom when his cock softened. With it taken care of, he returned to snuggle.

Jackie drifted in the blissful haze for a while before sleep took her.

* * * *

Jackie's phone trilled and vibrated against the base of the lamp, creating a piercing, clanking racket.

Groaning, she yanked the pillow over her head, but her phone was undeterred and the resounding clatter just wouldn't abate. Finally, she grabbed it. Her first thought was that it would disturb Logan, but a quick look over to his side of the bed found it empty.

The phone vibrated in Jackie's hand, a reminder that someone was insistent on contacting her. Caroline's name flashed on the screen, as did the time. It had to be important for her friend to be calling her so early.

Heart galloping, she swiped the screen. "Caroline? What's wrong?"

"Why aren't you answering your door?"

Jackie caught the hitch in her friend's voice. "Are you crying?" She tapped the button for loudspeaker and dropped it onto the bed as she searched for her clothes. "Give me five minutes and I'll meet you outside on the beach."

There was hesitance then a sniff. "All right."

Jackie hung up and ran around the room trying to gather everything together as quickly as she could.

"You weren't trying to ditch me, were you?" Logan walked in with a tray of what smelled like a delicious breakfast.

She barely paused to look at him. "I thought *you* ditched me, but no. Caroline called. She's upset about something."

Absolutely unimpressed, he sighed. "What now? Did she break a nail?"

Jackie gave him a withering glance as she slipped on her jeans and T-shirt. "It sounded bad."

"Right. I'm sure whatever it is, is apocalyptically horrible," he deadpanned. He put the tray on the bed as he shook his head. "Things haven't changed with you two, then. Caroline calls, and you go running."

Jackie ran her fingers through her hair and wound it at the back of her head into a bun. "It's not like that."

He pointedly looked her up and down. "Really? Because it looks exactly like that."

She wasn't about to explain herself to him. "Go ahead and judge, Logan. You always were above everyone, weren't you?"

"You know what I'm saying is the truth. She's always had you wound around her little finger."

Jackie turned to face Logan, almost stepping toe to toe with him as she glared. "You don't know what you're talking about."

"Why, because I'm not of the same breeding and I don't run in the same social circles, so I wouldn't understand?"

Again she was transported back, and not in a good way. "Logan. Stop. Just stop." She took a deep breath. "She's my friend and she's in distress. I have to go."

"Fine."

Jackie wasn't sure what she saw in his gaze, not that she had the brain power to waste on trying to figure him out. The intricacies of his mind had always been a bit of a mystery to her. It worked at lightning speed and made connections she would never make. Though he never seemed able to see things the way she did either.

And right now, she didn't have the time.

"I'll see you when I see you, I guess."

"Sure."

Jackie walked out, a little disappointed that he didn't follow her or try harder to stop her. She shook off the ridiculous feeling and stalked her way to the elevator then down to the beach.

Caroline waited for her two steps away from the sand, dressed to perfection despite the pallor in her cheeks and her red-rimmed eyes. She even made crying look good.

Jackie dashed over and hugged her. "Are you okay? What's going on?" Had Charles done something? She would chew him out if he had.

"I'm freaking out."

"About?"

"Getting married, of course." Caroline grabbed her arm and started walking. "I don't know how people can seem so happy while going through this. I'm petrified. Unless I'm the only one freaking."

"I'm sure everyone goes through this. It's just cold feet. You and Charles love each other. You're just stressed out over everything."

"I guess you're right. It doesn't help me in the meantime, though, does it?" She tittered nervously. "Is it too early for a cocktail?"

Jackie shook her head. "You're the bride. This is your week. If you want one, have one. Just don't go overboard."

"We just have to find somewhere to get one this early in the morning."

Jackie was glad a little color had returned to her friend's cheeks. "I'm sure someone will be willing to serve us a mimosa or two."

They walked along the waterline for a little while before Caroline asked the question Jackie had been dreading.

"Where were you this morning?"

Jackie hadn't had a chance to think of an excuse so she came up with the first thing that came to mind. "I was at the pool."

She studied Jackie a moment. "Really? Because your hair isn't wet."

"I just got there. I was getting changed when you called."

Caroline simply nodded, a frown marring her features. "Sorry about that."

"No worries." Jackie sagged with relief only to tense up again at her friend's next question.

"What happened after Logan dragged you out of the restaurant?" She held up her perfectly manicured hand. "No. What made him think he had the right to drag you out of there in the first place?"

"I have no idea, but he said it was because he didn't like how people were talking to — or, rather, *about* me."

Caroline raked her hands through her hair, letting her frustration shine through the calm she was trying so hard to achieve. "Should I point out to him that he's not your boyfriend anymore? And that their curiosity about you is his fault in the first place?"

That was the last thing she needed. "Totally unnecessary." The less he knew about her life, the less he would be inclined to meddle.

"I hope it's because you already told him off."

"Oh, I did." Guilt twanged in her chest.

Caroline sighed. "Then why do I get the feeling you're not telling me everything?"

"There's nothing to tell. He dragged me out, I told him off. End of story."

This time the sigh was approving. "Good. You don't want him ruining your life again."

As if anyone had to remind her of that that. Jackie stared out at the beach glumly. Was she just setting herself up for another big fall? Not if they kept things about the present. Bringing up past hurts would be pointless. She'd gotten over the situation — and Logan — and had carved a life out for herself. One that she was proud of.

Jackie wasn't looking for his apologies or approval.

Just his body for a little while.

If he was still willing. After the way they'd parted this morning, Logan might not exactly be amenable. But if the quality of the sex factored into the equation, he would welcome her back in a heartbeat. Jackie knew she wanted to get skin to skin with him again as soon as possible.

They walked along the sand for a while as they headed back to the hotel and walked into the nearest restaurant for breakfast and the mimosas they had been talking about. Which led to masterfully prepared Bellinis.

By the time the glasses were empty and the plates cleared away, Caroline's concerns had evaporated and so had a few of Jackie's.

Caroline stood a little unsteadily but managed to stay upright. "I have a few things I should see to. You're welcome to join me, if you'd like."

"I don't want to get in the way. Besides, I still have the pool to check out."

"I won't get in the way of that again." Caroline pulled her in for a hug. "Thanks for coming down and talking to me."

"What are friends for?"

Caroline tittered nervously. "Well, I hope you feel that way the rest of the week because I can't guarantee that I won't have another minor freak-out."

"And I'll be here for you. I'll see you later." Jackie squeezed her friend in another hug.

As she walked away, Caroline stopped and turned and teetered back. "Remember all the bridesmaids are meeting in the spa later."

She *had* forgotten. With everything going on, Jackie could stand a little pampering to get her mind off things. "I'll be there."

Caroline pecked her on the cheek and, doing her impression of a newborn fawn, carefully picked her way up the path farther into the building.

Not feeling any steadier than her friend, Jackie opted to stay by the aquarium to watch the fish. Taking the closest chair, she sat back and watched the rainbow-hued fish streak past the glass, darting in and out of the coral and dodging the streams of morning light. It was something she could easily lose herself in for hours.

"So you go running to her and she just leaves you here?"

Jackie sighed at Logan's voice. "It's not like that. I chose not to go with her." She turned to glare at him. "And why do I have to explain myself to you?"

"You don't. I just want you to think about how people treat you." He sat next to her and stared at the fish. "Twice now, I've seen people take advantage of you, talk about you like some toy, and you just take it."

"I appreciate your concern, but it's none of your business. Once we leave this place, you'll forget all about me again and how people treat me."

Logan grasped her hand in his, prompting her to meet his eyes. "If you think I could ever forget about you, you're wrong."

The sensation of his warm skin against hers, as he used to do all the time, brought forth some powerful emotions. Jackie severed the connection by quickly yanking her hand out of his. She wobbled a bit in her chair from the force of her movement. "We both know that's not true."

He eyed her angrily before it turned into something that looked like amusement. "Are you drunk?"

"Don't be ridiculous. I only had a couple of mimosas…and Bellinis."

"Geez, Jackie. It's not even nine a.m." He caught her when she listed a little too far to the right. "Still a lightweight, huh?"

"Caroline had cold feet. A few cocktails with breakfast seemed in order."

His smirk turned into a beaming smile. "For you, half a glass is more than enough."

She knew he was thinking of the time she'd gotten drunk off a single glass of champagne. It had been Christmas, and Logan had bought a bottle to celebrate. He'd even made dinner — or something that he'd called dinner. It had been one of the sweetest things he'd done. And she had promptly ruined it by downing the glass too fast and falling asleep almost immediately after the alcohol had worked into her system. Logan had teased her about it for months afterward, not to mention kept a close eye on her whenever they'd shared a drink.

"Want to walk it off?"

Walking probably wasn't a good idea just yet. "I think I'm good here for the moment."

"Need anything to eat?"

She let out an amused breath. "Believe it or not, Caroline and I had something to eat with the drinks."

He chuckled. "So we'll just sit and stare at the fish."

"You don't have to. I'm sure you have better things to do. Doesn't Charles need you for anything?"

"I'm sure he can survive without me. He's got, what, five other groomsmen?"

Jackie giggled. "Who needs that many?"

"I agree. Why would anyone want to put on such a big show? It's a commitment between two people. They're the only ones who should be there."

Once upon a time, Jackie had daydreamed about marrying Logan. All different scenarios had flitted through her mind. Grand weddings with dozens of bridesmaids, groomsmen and flower girls all the way to an intimate affair with just the two of them and someone to officiate. She had to admit that the small, quiet one had appealed to her more than any other. Jackie had pictured the two of them marrying on a beach at sunset the most often.

Logan's deep voice broke through her reverie. "Imagining something nice?"

"Just thinking."

Thinking about what? Or whom? Jackie wouldn't have that dreamy look on her face if she was thinking about him. Would she?

Did she have another man in her life?

No. Jackie would never have gotten into bed with him if she had. She'd never been that kind of girl. At least she hadn't in the past. She couldn't have changed that much, could she?

The thought of her with someone else gnawed at his gut. Logan knew he had no right to feel that way, but there was a primal part of him deep down that coveted Jackie and probably always would. She had been his everything, once. And was still incredibly compatible with him in bed.

The idea of her being just as willing and wonderful in bed with another man dropped a red haze over his vision.

"Logan? Is something wrong?" Jackie watched him with a strange expression on her face. All at once quizzical, amused and a little bit tipsy. "You look like you want to strangle someone."

"Do I?" Logan ran his fingertips over her cheek, dragging them down her neck the way he knew she liked. "Because I was thinking you owe me a morning after."

Color instantly flushed her cheeks, so he knew she remembered their mornings together. It might not have happened as often as he'd liked, but they would most often share breakfast after — sometimes before — making love again. One thing he had wished they could have done was spend all day in bed, but with classes, his work and her family, it had been a struggle to find time to be together.

It wasn't too late to realize that wish to spend the day together naked now.

"There was one thing I wanted to do while we were together that we never got to do."

Jackie's eyes had a mischievous glint to them when she looked at him. "Just one?"

He chuckled as he traced her collarbone. "Okay, one of the big ones."

"Well? What is it?"

Jackie looked open to whatever he would say so he went for it. "Spending the day with you. Naked."

He watched as the pupils of her eyes dilated almost as if she could see what he was imagining.

"So are you game?"

Jackie weighed his question carefully. It was like a blow to the gut as he thought about how she would have leaped at the chance when they were together.

"I should keep myself available for Caroline…"

It pissed him off that she was still putting Caroline's needs over his.

The resentment evaporated when Jackie smiled at him as she wound her arms around his neck.

"It's my vacation too, so I don't see why we couldn't. She can call if she needs me."

He couldn't help the grin. "Want some help?" He held out his hand to her.

Jackie slipped hers into his and hopped down from the chair.

Logan kissed the back of her hand as they started walking. He made sure to keep the pace slow, even though all he wanted to do was run straight back up to his suite. He wanted her to work the alcohol out of her system first. That and he wanted to get a handle on the emotion that burned in his chest. He didn't want it, but having Jackie spend time with him was like a blessing. It shouldn't have felt that way.

Logan didn't want to dwell on it now. Not while he had her with him and willing.

Jackie was far from being utterly incapacitated, but he wanted her fully aware and able to enjoy. The perfect place to take her came to mind.

"Why don't we take a little detour?"

Curiosity lit up her features. "To where?"

"I'm guessing you haven't had a chance to explore the hotel and its facilities yet."

"You'd guess right. Between arriving and… Well… I haven't had much of an opportunity to check this place out." Jackie looked up at him quizzically. "I'm guessing you have?"

"You could say that. It's a bit of a walk, though. Do you think you're up for it?" He hoped it was enough of a trek to help burn off the alcohol by the time they got there.

"I am if you are."

Jackie had always had an adventurous streak. It was one of the things they'd had in common and was the reason for the large number of unusual places they'd had sex.

They'd had quite a list. And now they'd be able to add to it.

The only tough part was deciding where first.

He was sure they'd figure it out as they went. "How long are you here for?"

She carefully kept her eyes on the scenery. "Just a few days."

There was something Jackie wasn't saying. She could stay as long as she liked. Obviously, she had something more important to get back to. Or she wanted to limit their time together.

It annoyed him that he wanted to know which. And that he wanted to know more about her life. More about her. Where had she been? What had she done? Who had she done it with? It was enough to drive him crazy.

After she'd left that morning, he'd thrown out the breakfast and burned out his frustration with laps in the pool.

It hadn't helped. He wanted her so badly his entire body ached. Logan's assumption that she felt the same way was obviously wrong. Yet another thing that pissed him off.

Chapter Six

Jackie studied Logan with covert glances. He was angry, but then what else was new? Since she'd first seen him in the hotel lobby, he'd looked incensed. The only time he hadn't was when they were naked. Or directly afterward.

But then who could look angry while they were having the kind of sex they were?

She absentmindedly rubbed her hands over the goosebumps the images brought to her arms. Everything between them might have been different, but—if anything—the sex had only gotten better. Though it could have been the fact that she had endured a really long dry spell after Logan.

It didn't change the fact that just thinking about him and what he could do to her got her wet.

He led her outside along several pathways that ran farther into the lush greenery. Jackie felt as though she was trekking through a dense jungle. Well, almost. The carefully constructed passageway they followed certainly helped facilitate their trek.

It dawned on her that they had been skirting the outside of the mountain quite high. Where on earth could he be leading her?

She trusted him enough not to take her somewhere dangerous and to give her what she needed in bed, but that was about as far as it went.

They continued to walk in silence, as he brooded over whatever it was he was focused on, meanwhile, she did her best not to give into her curiosity and ask. It was one rule she wasn't going to break. She didn't need to know, nor did she care.

Except she did, a little.

Jackie wanted to know more about where he'd been the past few years. After blocking the mere thought of him from her mind for so long, she realized there was so much about him that she wanted to know. So much she'd missed out on.

Gritting her teeth, she forced her focus onto everything but him.

The scents from the exotic plants were sweetly strange and wonderful. Flowers blended with the smell of the rocks, the moss and the other vegetation to create an intoxicating mix that she never wanted to forget. The cloying humidity thickened the air and clung to her clothes and skin, but whenever a breeze blew over it, the sudden chill would bring welcome respite, if only for a little while.

The physical activity cleared her head, however. The air and the scenery helped as well.

The incredibly long pathway led farther up and around the mountain peak until it leveled out for a few feet. Then the sloped turned into stone hugging stairs that seemingly descended into the mountain itself.

"Are you steady enough for this?"

Jackie studied the steps. On the one hand, she was slightly concerned at not knowing where they were going. On the other, the mystery had her itching to find out. She nodded brusquely. "If we take it slow. I'll let you know if I get into any trouble."

Logan nodded. "Right. I'll go first. You can use me to break your fall if it comes to it."

So nice that he had such faith in her abilities. She kept the sarcasm to herself and followed. He would make a suitable cushion if she needed it.

With each step downward, Jackie could almost feel a perceptible drop in temperature. Too bad they didn't have that far to go.

Logan stopped her while the route was still enveloped by vegetation.

"What is it?" Had he spotted something dangerous?

"Close your eyes."

"You're kidding, right?" After making sure to be so careful with her, now he wanted her to follow him blind?

"I've got you. Don't worry. Just keep them closed until I tell you."

The hopeful little smile on his face was the impetus she needed to follow directions. With a sigh and what she hoped was a withering last glance at him, she let her eyes fall closed.

Logan linked his large hand with hers securely before he slowly led the way.

"Careful, there's one last step."

But instead of letting her take it, he lifted her in his arms and navigated it himself.

Sunshine warmed her skin as her feet touched the softest sand she'd ever encountered and sank into it. Logan carefully turned her around and whispered, "Open your eyes."

When she did, her gaze immediately fell upon crystalline blue water and pristine white sand, only on a much smaller scale than the hotel's beach front. The horseshoe-shaped beach curved, almost meeting where sea water entered through a gap in the mountains.

"Wow!"

Jackie immediately strode to the water. Kicking off her sandals, she let the little waves lap at her toes.

"This is incredible." She watched the tiny ripples on the almost still surface.

"It is. There's a volcanic spring on the other side of the island as well. We could check that out sometime."

Jackie grinned at him. "I'm guessing this is hotel property?" She looked up and down the little beach, but aside from a few tables and lounge chairs, she couldn't see any other signs of life. At least not human. Birds sang, unseen in the vegetation, but there was nothing else.

"It is. And if you're expecting to see other people, you won't find any. They don't usually open this up until the evening." He pointed to a little alcove not too far away. "There's a bar in there and a sound system."

"So this is a party beach." It was amazing how pristine they managed to keep it. "I'm impressed with how well they maintain the area. It's practically untouched."

"That's the idea. They work hard at it, I'm sure."

She raised her eyebrows at him questioningly. "How do you know so much about this place?"

Logan smiled teasingly. "No questions, remember? Just accept that I know and use it to your advantage."

"And how would I do that?"

He tapped his fingers to his lips. "Well, if I were you, I would ask the incredibly handsome man you're with how long we'd be alone."

Rolling her eyes, she played along. "So how long before the partying hordes descend?"

"We have more than enough time to do this."

Without another word, he peeled off his shirt. Before she could protest, he dropped his shorts as well, giving her an unabashed view of his stunning body.

Logan really wasn't playing fair.

A wicked grin on his face, he turned and dashed for the water. He dove into the clear lake, disappearing for a long while before he resurfaced with the wide smile still on his face.

"What are you waiting for?"

Shaking her head, Jackie tugged off her clothes then ran in after him. It was surreal, but it felt great to be so reckless and carefree.

The warmth of the water surprised her. It was like diving into a giant, beautifully staged bath. When she broke through the surface again to refill her lungs, she found Logan smiling back at her. For the first time since they'd been reacquainted, he looked truly happy.

"So all it took to put a smile on your face was to go skinny dipping with you?"

"I could say the same about you." Logan splashed her. "Though you do seem to lose the scowl whenever I get naked."

She splashed him back. "I was going to say."

"Can you blame me? Look at you. Why wouldn't seeing you naked put a smile on my face?"

Jackie fought the urge to sink a little lower, not that it would help, since she could see straight to the bottom. She was more interested in seeing *him* naked.

"Will you explain to me the purpose of skinny dipping?"

He smirked. "To get the girl naked."

"I guess that's that then." Jackie turned to head back toward the shore.

Logan lunged. He quickly grabbed her around the waist and dragged her back.

"Not so fast. That's the initial intent. After that, it's a crap shoot. Things might happen, things might not. There may be begging involved. It all depends on the situation."

She burst out laughing. Why did it have to be Logan that made her feel so happy and carefree?

He wrapped his arms around her, a big grin on his own face.

"Now this is my idea of a vacation. I've got you, an island, five-star accommodation... This is paradise."

It was nice to hear, though she was pretty sure that she could be substituted with any other woman.

Instead of focusing on the strange feeling that thought left in her gut, she concentrated on the sensation of his solid body against hers.

"I'm liking the muscles."

He laughed. "You make it sound like I was a wimp back then."

"Not at all. You've just filled out." And he looked better than she'd imagined. He'd obviously been working out. But for whose benefit?

The pang of jealousy gnawed at her. The thought of another woman with Logan didn't settle well, even though she knew what was between them had been over for years. What they shared now was purely physical and nothing more. There was simply no reason she should feel one way or the other about anything to do with Logan.

"What's the matter?"

"Aren't you worried that we might get caught? We can't have that much time here alone before someone else discovers this place."

He wiggled his eyebrows at her as he tugged her closer. "We'd better get to the fun bit then."

Jackie clung to him as he stepped into deeper water, using his superior height to his advantage. Not that it was any hardship for her.

He was hard against her. Jackie clearly felt his erection already huge and ready.

She wrapped herself around him, gripping his hips with her thighs, bringing him in contact with her aching core.

"Not going to beg?" The joke left her lips on a sigh.

Logan gripped her hips and slid himself against her. The delicious friction sent shivers of delight skittering up her spine.

"If you want me to beg, I'm more than willing."

The thought of Logan begging her had its merits. "Please do."

He lowered his head to kiss her neck. The hot, open-mouthed caresses heated her skin, radiating waves of pleasure from the spot his lips touched.

"Please…"

Logan captured her lips before he repeated the move, grazing her intimately with his cock.

"May I…?"

He licked her bottom lip before sucking it between his and gave her a kiss she felt from the top of her head down to the tips of her toes. Logan drew his head back as he butted the head of his cock against her slit.

"Fuck you until you come screaming in my arms?"

Oh God.

It was on the tip of her tongue to say yes. It would have been so much easier to let her body do the talking and just to sink onto him, but he wasn't wearing a condom. And even worse, there were faint voices approaching.

Logan must have heard them too, because he pushed her toward the shore. "Head to the cave."

Jackie didn't have to be told twice. She swam as quickly as she could and dashed onto the sand and into the dark hollow in the mountainside. Peeking around the rock, she watched as Logan reached their clothes, snatched them up and ran along the beach to join her.

The whole situation was just so ludicrous she couldn't help the giggles that bubbled out of her. Only with Logan did things like this happen to her and for some reason it was fun, exciting.

Logan dashed in, snaring her by her waist then holding her tight against him as he scanned the scene for the newcomers. It seemed another couple had the same idea as Logan had.

The other pair reached the beach and quickly stripped down. The slightly paunchy man dragged the fiery-haired woman into the water with him. They didn't waste any time as they started exploring each other. He clumsily pawed her breasts and ass, not that she seemed to mind. She giggled as if he was making her day. They got about waist deep before he picked her up and wrapped her legs around his waist as they kissed passionately.

While it was obvious that they were about to witness an X-rated scene, neither Jackie nor Logan moved away.

As she watched the other couple's heated embrace, she felt Logan's renewing interest against her ass. He grazed his teeth over her shoulder then dragged his lips to her neck. Logan nibbled lightly on her earlobe before kissing his way down to her shoulder blade. His touch was light, dancing over her skin, coaxing goosebumps all over her. Excitement shortened her breath until it came in quick pants.

She heard him rummaging through their clothes a second before he dropped them. Then the telltale sound of a condom wrapper tear as he sheathed himself. Were they really going to have sex while watching another couple? The decadent thrill sent shivers skittering through her. The closest they'd come to doing this in the past had been watching themselves in a mirror. That had been hot. This? The naughty buzz only added to the heat already flaring deep inside her.

He closed one hand around one of her breasts, kneading gently while he glided the other down her side, then he changed its trajectory to cup her mound. Jackie spread her legs, allowing him better access, and Logan immediately sought her clit, rubbing small circles.

Jackie's legs wobbled, and she had to bite her lip in an attempt to keep her cries quiet.

"You think he can do the same to her?" Logan rasped. "Do you think he can make her squeal and tremble just by using his fingers?"

It wasn't until then that Jackie realized her eyes had closed as she savored the pleasure his touch evoked. The other couple were back on shore now and were engaged in very passionate sex as the water lapped at their legs.

Logan slipped his fingers inside her, crooking them as he drew them out only to plunge them deeply again. "Do you think he can get her just as wet as I get you? That he can make her legs unsteady with just a touch?"

She doubted it. Jackie watched the other woman arch under the man. She clearly enjoyed what he was doing to her.

The head of Logan's cock grazed her ass as he pressed it between her legs and slid into her with a series of short thrusts, eliciting gasps from Jackie each time.

Logan's voice was heavy with lust. "He's not working with what I've got, but she seems to like it well enough."

Breathless, Jackie arched back against him. She didn't care what the other two were doing. All that mattered was reaching her goal of a shattering climax. *Now.*

"Think I can get you to come before he can get her there?" He withdrew almost completely before he thrust hard, drawing another mewling cry from Jackie.

Think? She knew she would. A few more thrusts and the continued toying of her clit would get her there in seconds, if he would stop playing around, and he knew it.

"Logan, please." The words came on a moan. She pushed back against him, meeting his thrusts, magnifying each impact.

Logan chuckled as he lowered his head to the crook of her neck. "I love it when you beg me." His thrusts were languid, though deep and penetrating.

Jackie's breath caught. She wound her arm around his neck, anchoring his lips in place. "Shut up and prove you can out do that guy."

With a chuckle, he moved in earnest now, his driving strokes rocking her entire body.

As predicted, the pleasure crested quickly and spiked after only a few strokes. Fireworks exploded behind her eyelids as she cried out. The sensation was too great. There was no way she could contain it. Nor did she care to. Logan clamped his hand over her mouth as he pushed her over the precipice and continued to drive into her, seeking his own release.

His pounding rhythm compounded the sensations propelling her to another orgasm more devastating than the first that racked her from head to toe.

Behind her, Logan groaned as he thrust deep, jerking his hips as he sagged against her.

It took a long while for her vision to clear and for her to come back to herself. Logan held her gently, keeping her from collapsing against the rough stone. It had been hard and fast and amazing, so Jackie wasn't prepared for the laughter that rumbled through him.

"What's so funny?" Was he amused at how easily he could make her come? She immediately sought her clothes.

Logan took her hands, ceasing her movement. "Look." He pointed at the scene on the beach.

The other couple had already gotten most of their clothes on and, from the scowl on the woman's face, she hadn't quite gotten what she was looking for. The slumped shoulders and sheepish apologetic look on the man's face filled in the rest of the story.

She dropped her head to Logan's shoulder as she tried to hold back the laughter. "That poor woman." She probably had sand in some terrible places and without the payoff of an orgasm. That would rankle just about anyone.

Not every man was Logan in the sack, and didn't she know it.

They got dressed in silence and waited until the other couple were long gone before leaving their hiding place.

Jackie seemed to be deep in thought but he didn't want to ask what she was thinking. Whatever it was didn't seem good. If there was anything he remembered about her it was that she liked to be left alone to brood.

He simply took her hand and held it loosely as they walked a meandering path back to the hotel. So far their reunion had been surprising. There had been a time he hoped they would come together again and this had proved to be everything he had hoped it would be. But there was something else lurking beneath the surface, and he knew he had to be careful or he'd find himself falling for her all over again.

Sex in the cave had been hot. The other couple showing up had been completely unexpected, but it hadn't dulled what had happened between them. Not that he'd anticipated anything less. But simply seeing what had transpired between the other two drove home just how good things were between Jackie and himself.

At least that one part of their relationship. He couldn't let himself forget what she'd done to him. That this whole thing was about getting revenge and eventually closure on the Jackie chapter of his life.

Another thing he had to make sure was that she didn't fall for him as well. As much as he hated what had happened between them and her part in it, the more time spent with her reminded him that she was a truly good person. He was torn between wanting revenge and just walking away.

They had a few days left. Did he really want to lose out on more time with her? Who was he kidding? He didn't want to miss out on some stellar sex.

He was already getting hard again just thinking about the word in conjunction with Jackie.

"What do you have planned for today?" Logan sincerely hoped it had something to do with him and varying degrees of nakedness.

"Nothing, really. I had wanted to explore some more and maybe spend some time in my pool."

Her pool, huh? "Want company? I haven't got much to do either."

"Didn't you say you were here on business as well as for the wedding?"

Damn. She was right. One night with Jackie and his brain had already turned to mush. He looked up at the sky. The sun was quite high, so he assumed it was nearing noon. He smirked at Jackie. "I... Yeah. I do have a few things to take care of this afternoon, but I can meet you afterward."

"Sure." She frowned. "I forgot. Caroline said something about the bridesmaids meeting at the spa today, so if you can't find me, I'll probably be there."

Logan nodded. "Great. See you later." He leaned in to kiss her on reflex but stopped himself, feigning picking something out of her hair. "You had a bit of something."

The smile she gave him looked forced. "Thanks." Jackie let go of his hand, leaving him staring at her ass and the way it swayed as she walked.

He rubbed the back of his head. She was amazing.

* * * *

Logan hurried into the meeting room after having returned to his room for a quick shower and change of clothes. He hated being back in a suit, especially in the heat and humidity. Thankfully, as far as he knew, they were going to stay within the blissfully air-conditioned building.

The men he was to meet were already there. The one at the center of the group noticed him first and parted the small crowd to greet him with an extended hand. "Logan. Good to see you again."

"Mr. Foster." He shook his hand then those of the other men one after another.

"We were just going to go down to the bar. This room might be perfect for a board meeting, but I prefer a more informal setting."

"Of course. And you'll get to see some of the hotel at the same time."

Bradley Foster strode ahead leading the pack of suits through the hall and into the foyer. He paused and looked to Logan.

He smiled and took the lead. "Follow me."

It grew into a true grin when he walked into the bar and saw the spot where he and Jackie had danced the night before. He quickly wiped the expression off his face and turned to the men. "Here we are."

"Excellent." Foster waved at the bartender and pointed to a nearby table. He received a nod and he led the way.

They each took a seat, made their orders and got down to business.

"So, Logan, you handle the security for this resort."

It wasn't a question.

Logan nodded. "I designed the system, yes."

"Impressive."

The waiter appeared and distributed the drinks, putting a pause on their conversation for a few moments. The guy smiled and headed back to the bar.

Logan was the only one to order a non-alcoholic drink. The reason behind it wasn't because he was in the middle of a business meeting—he could handle his drink as well as anyone at the table—but he wanted to be hydrated and ready for his meet-up with Jackie later.

If anyone noticed his choice of drink, no one mentioned it.

"We have a resort planned and it will need a great amount of security. We foresee a playground for the wealthy and that requires a certain amount of discretion as well as reassurance of their safety. After what we've seen here so far, we certainly consider you to be a forerunner for the position."

"Thank you." Logan was gratified that his work had finally put him on the map. After years of chasing down prospects and convincing them that he was the one for the job, they were finally coming to him. "I assure you that if you choose me for the job, you will be nothing but happy with the result."

There were nods and smiles from around the table as the men settled back to talk and drink.

"We'll be staying for the next few days to get a feel for what you do. Look around and whatnot. We should be able to make our decision by then."

"Great."

The conversation turned to chitchat and Logan found he wasn't nearly as interested as he should have been in what they were talking about. He couldn't focus on them when his mind kept wandering back to Jackie.

She had mentioned the spa. All the things they could get up to in there were mind-boggling. Logan pieced together a plan that would enable them to do just that.

* * * *

Jackie lay prone on the cushioned table, her face in the little hole, as she listened to the relaxing music. Caroline and the rest of the women had opted for facials while Jackie had figured a massage would do her wonders. Not that the fantastic sex she and Logan had been having had had a detrimental effect on her physically. But she needed a break from all the stressing out over what she had been doing, about the man himself. Over their past. Over what the hell she was doing with him.

She didn't want to admit it, but the attraction to him was stronger than ever. And the sex? Even more mind-blowing. And now she was becoming addicted again. She just needed to take a moment and get a grip on reality.

They didn't have a relationship. They were two consenting adults having a good time and nothing more. She had to remember that. Jackie couldn't afford to lose herself in him again. A little perspective was all she needed.

She'd spent pretty much the entire time in the spa so far obsessing over it. All the giggling and gossip over mani-pedis did little to distract her.

So Jackie had snuck away for a massage.

The door opened.

"Miss Pennington. Sorry for the wait, we'll start in just a moment."

"That's fine."

"Are you comfortable?"

"I am." If it wasn't for the thoughts running rampant in her mind, she probably would have fallen asleep by now. Between the heavenly scents, the music and the cushy table, it was perfectly relaxing.

"I'll start with your legs and work my way up. If anything is uncomfortable or if you would like me to stop for any reason, just let me know."

"I will." She let her eyes drift closed as his hands closed over her legs and gently began kneading her tense muscles.

Slowly, he made his way up her legs. First the right then the left. He carefully and expertly manipulated what felt like every muscle in his path.

Jackie couldn't help the sigh that escaped. The man's hands were magic and only slightly edged out Logan's by a hair.

What would it be like to have Logan massage her? For his size, he was gentle with her, unless they were both in the mood for something a little rougher. He'd given her the odd backrub here and there, though the chemistry between them was so incendiary that almost every occasion had quickly escalated into something more before he could make it away from her torso.

She imagined his strong hands would have no problem smoothing away any aches and pains.

As the masseur's ministrations traveled higher up her thigh, she envisaged they were Logan's. His caress would get lighter, more teasing as he reached the curve of her ass. Logan would slide his hand over it. Maybe he would grip it. Or perhaps he would be in a naughtier mood and he'd give it a light slap.

Jackie squirmed a little at the thought. An ache grew between her legs. She could only hope that the man wouldn't notice.

He worked on her thighs a little longer, probably having picked up on her tension. All she could think was that if Logan had been there they would make good use of the oils and the table. She imagined him behind her as he pressed her face first into the table, impaling her from behind. In another scenario he was under her, gleaming from the oils as she rode him.

As her mind wandered, she could have sworn the man's hand grazed her ass. It didn't happen again, so she put it down to her overactive imagination. He slid his hands slid up her back, aided by the slick oils, gliding them over her skin and creating a warm wake of sensation.

In her head, it was Logan touching her, and her body reacted accordingly. The hard tips of her breasts rubbed into the table seeking his touch. She knew that she was getting wetter and wetter by the second and was afraid to move lest the man realize what was going through her mind.

Willing her breathing to remain even, she bit her lip and did what she could to distract herself.

It didn't help when his hands were working such magic on her skin. His touch, now that she focused on it, was familiar. And as it got bolder and bolder a smile spread over her lips.

"Logan."

The towel covering her backside was torn aside and his greased hands eased over the skin there before giving her a stinging slap.

"I was wondering how long it was going to take you to figure it out," he growled. "I can smell you. You're fucking well turned on."

Jackie turned over to face him. "Because I was imagining you were the one touching me and what we could be doing if you were here with me."

"Oh, yeah?" Biting his lush bottom lip, he crossed his arms and stared down at her, clearly exploring her with his eyes. The mischievous glint in them told her he was using his own imagination now as well. "What would you do to me?"

She batted her lashes coquettishly at him. "Well, first you would give me an amazing massage like you were doing. Only it would take a slightly more X-rated turn."

"I'm liking it so far."

"Once I'm all oiled up and possibly still shaking from an orgasm or two, it's your turn." Telling him what she was thinking only increased the delicious tension in her and she knew Logan loved it when she was vocal about what she wanted. "I'll rub it all over and into your skin, concentrating on the part of you that seems to want out." She let her eyes drop to the straining bulge at his groin and smiled. "I tend to get very distracted when he comes out to play, however."

"I'll just have to take up the slack then, won't I?"

Exactly what she hoped he'd say.

Logan took off his clothes with precise and deliberate movements then donned a condom in record time. Instead of massaging her as she'd expected, he dragged her toward him so he stood between her thighs. He stretched his long arm out, allowing him to close his hand around a bottle, which he brought back and tipped over her breasts. He watched with utter fascination as the oil slicked over her.

After putting the glass container down, he quickly returned his hands to her skin, smoothing and rubbing the luxuriously scented oil over her breasts. Once satisfied they were sufficiently oiled, he guided his hands lower over the slight swell of her belly and over her thighs.

Much of the oil had pooled between them where he was tightly wedged against her.

He slipped his thumb between them, using it to simultaneously drip the oil lower and circle her clit.

Jackie let out a mewling cry as he grazed her sensitive folds first with his fingers then with the broad head of his cock. She could easily orgasm from that alone. Logan knew exactly where to touch her and with how much pressure to make her explode.

He grinned at Jackie when her breath hitched—he knew she was close. Logan dragged himself over her again before he found the right spot and buried himself inside her.

Jackie clung to him as best she could as he set a fast, hard rhythm. The oil added another level to his penetration, easing his way, changing the feel of the friction. The slippery-slick sensation was incredible.

The squelching squish it made whenever their bodies met upped the decadent thrill as he took everything she had to give. Logan leaned forward, bouncing her under him, rubbing her breasts against the roughness of his chest. The combination of coarse and lubricious was amazing. Logan seemed to enjoy it just as much as she was. He held her gaze. Absolutely focused. Utterly intent on making her burn up before he blew.

His breath came in hot pants against her cheek as he whispered, "Come for me, Jackie. I need to feel you coming around me."

His rough entreaty spiked her pleasure. It took her another handful of thrusts to completely come apart.

Logan closed his mouth over hers, to keep her cries from drawing attention as he pounded into her. Hands convulsing on her hips, he held her in place, shoving himself as deeply as he could into Jackie. Pulling out and doing it again and again until he shouted into her mouth and his body shuddered against hers.

She stared at him. He was a handsome man but he was never more beautiful to her than in the moments just after he came. There was something about the vulnerability and the calmness in his eyes that drew her inexorably to him. He looked so peaceful when he usually seemed so determined, stressed.

Now was a prime example.

Jackie gazed at him and felt as though she was seeing the real him. The man she hadn't seen in a very long time. It wasn't to last.

He smiled at her tentatively before grabbing a couple of towels. "We should probably get out of here."

Damn. She'd forgotten where they were.

Jackie rubbed as much of the residue off her as she could before putting the robe back on. "Caroline is in the room next to us, I think. We're supposed to be spending a few hours getting pampered."

"She can have you for a few hours then. But will you meet me for dinner?"

"I don't see why not." Anything would be better than another meal with Caroline's and Charles' families. Dinner with Logan sounded heavenly. "I'll give her some excuse. Where do you want to meet? The restaurant?"

"I'll come get you."

"Great." She flipped her hair out of the collar of the robe. "How did you get in here anyway?"

Logan buttoned his shirt. "I just told the masseur that you're my girlfriend and to start, then I would take over. I sweetened the deal with a few bills and here we are."

Warmth punched her in the chest when he called her his girlfriend. "I can't believe you did that."

"What? Are you complaining?"

Far from it. "Not at all. It's just a lot of trouble to go to for sex."

"Not for the kind we have." He put his jacket back on and straightened the lapels.

Jackie licked her lips. He was right about that. "You should get out of here before Caroline sees you."

He lowered his eyebrows. "Are you worried about what she'll think?"

This was a conversation they'd had many times. She never could get him to see things from her point of view. Only this time things were different. They didn't have a relationship. He had run out on her once before. If her friend found out it would only lead to more questions, and she just didn't have the patience or the answers for her. How could she explain to Jackie what she was doing with Logan when she wasn't sure herself?

And to tell Caroline it was just sex would just go over her head. She just didn't work that way. She would never get past what Logan had done or that what they shared was so powerful that she didn't want to stop it.

Stupid, Jackie knew. But she just couldn't help herself.

"I'll take that as a yes." Logan glared at her. "Still afraid you're slumming it?"

Jackie sighed. "You sure know how to ruin a good mood, don't you?"

"Just give me an answer. You're ashamed to be seen with me. Always have been."

"The only one of us with a problem in that department was you, Logan." She stood and stepped closer. "I didn't care about that shit then and I don't care about it now. You were the one with the colossal chip on your shoulder. When we were together, I was so in love with you and I didn't care who knew it. You could have been the richest man or the poorest, and I wouldn't have cared. You were the love of my life." Gritting her teeth against the tears, she pushed past him. "Forget about dinner. And if you see Caroline, tell her I've got a migraine or something."

Jackie dashed from the room, fighting back tears as she ran. She didn't know what had come over her. Blurting all that out had definitely not been part of the plan. But his attitude, the one that obviously hadn't changed, had pissed her off. That he thought so little of her frustrated her to no end.

Swiping away her tears, Jackie reached her suite only to realize that she'd left her key card — as well as her clothes — back at the spa.

"I thought you might need these." Logan was walking up the hall with her clothes bundled in one hand.

Jackie ran her hands over her cheeks, wiping away what tears had escaped. She snatched the clothes away and dug through them for her card.

"I'm sorry."

She didn't spare him a glance. All she wanted was to get out of there and into her suite.

"Jackie, will you look at me?"

"There's nothing to say, Logan." She shrugged his hand off when he put it on her shoulder.

He grasped both shoulders this time and gently turned her around to face him. The contrite expression on his face seemed honest enough.

"I was being a dick. I admit it. I'm sorry."

"Yes, you were. Didn't you ever think that you were enough for me? That you were all I wanted?"

Logan sighed. "Can we do this inside?"

"Jackie? Are you okay?"

Caroline stomped her way up the hall and wedged herself between her and Logan. "What the hell are you doing here?" She looked at Jackie and her eyes narrowed when she saw Jackie's puffy eyes and tear stains. She pointed a finger at Logan. "Did you make her cry?"

He grit his teeth. "We were talking, Caroline."

Logan attempted to sidestep her irate friend, but she followed him, getting directly in his path.

"Just go, Logan." Jackie finally managed to get her card in the lock and pushed the door open.

"Fine. But we *have* to talk, Jackie."

He stalked away feeling shaken and a little hollow. Jackie's reaction, her words, had cut him to the quick.

It hadn't been an act. They hadn't been words hurled in anger. He knew what he'd seen. Jackie was hurting and that made his heart ache. If Caroline hadn't turned up he would have dragged Jackie into her room and done anything to take that haunted look off her face.

Not for the first time, he felt something was off with what had happened between them. He was more confused than ever now. Logan had been so sure that she had been the one to end their relationship. Had he gotten it wrong? If he had been the love of her life maybe she had been coerced into breaking up with him?

But if she didn't care about money or status, then who could have pushed her to do it, and for what? What could have possibly made her do it?

Logan kept walking as he pondered. Before long, he found himself at the bar. Why not have a drink as he did a little more thinking?

He ordered a beer and took the bottle with him to the balcony overlooking the water, stopping at the exact spot where he and Jackie had stood at before. Logan took a swig as he stared at the ocean. The stunning scenery was all but lost to him as he sifted through his memories.

Their time together had been great. They'd been so young, how could it not? While they'd had a few responsibilities, it had been nothing compared to life now, in the real world. They had spent as much time as possible together between classes and his part time job. It had been idyllic, almost dreamy. And then it had all come crashing down. That was the time he focused on. No matter how much it hurt him to remember.

He knew he had a chip on his shoulder about their different social classes. He always had. Jackie had never let him see it bother her, but he had been sure it had. She couldn't bring him home to meet her parents. He couldn't provide her with the kind of life she was accustomed to. It was yet another thing that had driven him crazy. Logan had done everything he could to make a little cash so he could splurge on her whenever he could. Those early days had been filled with plans and laying groundwork for his career in security software. The insecurity and the need to give Jackie everything she wanted had pushed him to become what he was now.

And it had been totally on him.

Jackie was right when she'd said he was the one with the problem.

So then what had happened? He had proposed. Logan had been pretty sure she was as thrilled as he was at the thought of getting married. Up until that night, there had been no indication otherwise. They'd bickered over trivial things but otherwise their relationship had been perfect.

Logan took another long pull of his beer.

Something had prompted her to send him away and he was going to find out what.

Chapter Seven

It had taken Jackie an hour to get Caroline to leave. The questions had been endless and there had been just as many accusations. Had he hurt her? Was he bullying her? What had he done to make her cry?

Caroline had been relentless.

Not that Jackie didn't appreciate her friend's concern, she just didn't like being treated like a helpless little girl.

Yes, Logan had devastated her the last time. Yes, it had taken everything she had to pick herself up and start again. But she had done it and without the help of anyone else. She could handle Logan. It was the fallout from being anywhere near him that was going to drive her insane. Not only was there the chemistry that crackled between them to navigate, but there were also old feelings—and not only from her and Logan—to deal with.

Jackie flopped onto her bed and stared at the net spread over her as a canopy.

It took her a long while to gather up the strength to get off the bed and wander through the room. As she approached the pool, she knew it would help her relax somewhat.

Jackie dropped the robe before she stepped into the cool water.

Bless whoever came up with the idea to equip all the rooms with infinity pools.

There was something so decadent about bathing nude out in the open where she knew that if someone tried hard enough they could see her.

Jackie didn't care. It was liberating, and wasn't that part of why she was there in the first place? She needed a break from her life. It wouldn't have mattered where she'd gone. In fact, she would have preferred to go somewhere more low-key. Where she wouldn't be reminded of her past. But there she was and she was determined to at least enjoy some of her time at the resort. Even if it was alone in her suite.

One simply didn't go to a Totally Five Star Hotel and sulk.

Jackie dove under and swam straight for the glass that stopped the water from flowing over the side of the mountain. She opened her eyes and peered through the thick barrier at the blurry world on the other side. It was like peeking into an alternate reality where things seemed familiar but it took her squinting and some imagination to get it to look right.

Flipping over onto her back, she closed her eyes, drifting in a personal cocoon of bliss. She smiled up at the sun as it warmed her skin. The stress evaporated under the glaring heat along with the water off her skin.

She dove again to return to floating on her back lazily, repeating the action every time her skin dried. And each time more and more of her worries drifted away. What she wouldn't give to have one of these back at home.

Jackie would have stayed in the water until she shriveled up like a raisin, but a knock at the door drew her out of her blissful world.

"Just a minute!"

Jackie noticed the chill in the air and the waning sunlight. How long had she been in the water?

She got out but sidestepped the oil-covered robe from the spa as she skidded her way to the bathroom in search of the complimentary robe that she knew would be in there.

"Jackie? Are you okay?"

It was Logan. Who else would it be?

"I'm good. Give me a sec." She shoved her arms into the robe and haphazardly tied it just as she opened the door.

Logan stood on the other side. He'd changed out of his oily clothes and stood before her in dark trousers and a white linen button-down.

"Hi."

Jackie nodded, waiting for him to tell her why he was there.

He gave her a somewhat lopsided smile. "I'm guessing Caroline's gone or I'd have her jumping down my throat right about now."

"It took some convincing, but I got her to believe that I wasn't going to fall apart." Jackie had meant the comment to be glib, but it came out more serious.

"I'm sorry about earlier." He peered over her shoulder. "Mind if I come in?"

She did mind. Very much so.

"I don't know if that's such a good idea. I'm not exactly dressed and I was thinking about ordering room service—"

"I'll join you."

"For some quality time with myself."

He smirked. "I promise not to pounce on you. I just want to talk. Spend some time together."

Jackie eyed him. He might have meant it at the moment, but when it came to the two of them it was way too easy to forget about intentions and fall into bed.

Logan held up his hand and gave her his most charming smile. "I swear. You could strip naked and climb all over me and nothing will happen."

Right. Not that she would. They could control themselves. They weren't animals.

"Come in." She stepped aside, and he walked in. Logan smelled amazing. Like cologne, a shower, spiced with the scent of him.

"Been in the pool?"

Letting the door close, she waved at her waterlogged self. "How could you tell?"

"Just a wild guess." He spun and looked at her accommodations. "Nice."

"Did you expect anything else?"

He shook his head. "Nope. But I had been wondering. It's not like I've been able to see every room in this place."

"I'm pretty sure they had luxury in mind when designing this entire hotel."

He nodded as he circled the space. "Yeah, I would say so. I would have thought you would have gotten a bigger suite, though."

"What? Like yours?" Chuckling, Jackie shrugged. "This is more than adequate."

"Shall I order us dinner?

"Sure. I'll get dressed."

It looked like it was on the tip of his tongue to say something, but he nodded.

Jackie jammed her arm into her suitcase and grabbed some clothes out of it without looking and retreated to the bathroom. "You know what I like."

She heard, "I certainly do," as the door swung closed.

Logan picked up the menu more to keep his hands busy than anything. He already knew what he would order after studying the menu when he'd been in his own suite contemplating the same thing. What he needed right now was a distraction from the naked woman not too far away.

At least she seemed better than when he had left her before. The paleness had gone and thankfully so had the tears. It tore at him to see her cry. Did he want to ask her what had happened and risk bringing her to tears again?

It wasn't what he wanted.

He'd have to feel her out. See where the conversation took them.

Logan picked up the phone and ordered.

Once that was done, he tapped on the door separating them. "I've made the order. It should be here soon."

"Right. I'll just be a few minutes."

"No problem." Logan circled the room again looking for a way of making it a bit more suitable for the type of meal he had in mind.

Tugging the sheets off the bed, he headed toward the pool, stopped just short of the opening and spread them over the wood. He returned to grab the pillows off the bed and the cushions from the couch and dropped them strategically on the sheets.

The effect was a picnic under the sunset without having to deal with grass or sand or bugs. Yet they still got the benefit of the fresh, cooling air and the sight of the stars.

By the time Jackie emerged, he had everything all laid out but the food. He'd found some candles and a lighter and had done what he could to make it look, well, pretty.

Jackie's gaze fell upon what he'd done and shook her head with an amused little smile. "What's going on in here?"

"I thought we could have a picnic." He held his hand out for her to take.

Jackie looked lovely in the pale yellow sundress. He could see she hadn't put on a bra and judging from the shadows he could see through the rather thin fabric, she probably hadn't put on panties either. He tore his gaze away to take in her hair, which was back up in a damp ponytail. She almost appeared like her younger self. Only the look in her eyes was different. Jackie dissected whatever she saw now, unlike her wide-eyed optimistic self before. What had caused that?

She slipped her hand into his and he led her to their impromptu picnic. Jackie sat, arranging her legs and skirt carefully, further convincing him that she didn't wear anything under the dress.

He'd had to go and make that stupid promise not to do anything.

Picturing her bare beneath the dress played havoc with his hormones. He had to keep his mind on the meal, the scenery, the room. Anything but Jackie.

He looked at the sky for a moment admiring the watercolor-like sunset of pinks and blues.

"So are we actually eating or are we having an imaginary feast?"

There was a knock at the door, and he pointed triumphantly at it. "Eating, of course."

He quickly crossed the space to answer the door. He greeted the waiter with a grin, took possession of the cart holding the massive tray and handed him a thick wad of bills before wishing him a good night and closing the door again.

With a proud grin, he wheeled it in next to Jackie, carefully took the tray off the top and placed it on the middle of the sheet, then dropped to sit next to her.

Jackie gave him an amused grin. "You look like a kid on Christmas morning."

He felt like it. At least a little.

Logan took a moment building up the anticipation before he lifted the lid with a flourish.

Underneath sat a six-course meal fit for royalty. As described on the menu there was smoked salmon cream topped with caviar, seared scallops served with Kobe beef and *kimchee*, foie gras with caramelized apple and an almond crust, crispy goats cheese morsels, red snapper with pearl couscous and champagne butter, dry-aged filet mignon with a purple potato cake and grilled pumpkin and finally dark chocolate and white chocolate truffles with a chocolate soufflé cake topped with raspberry Chantilly cream for dessert. Each plate came with a pair of complementing wines for them to enjoy. There was even an extra pair of glasses containing what looked like the pink champagne that came as the mid-meal drink described on the menu.

The chef and sommelier certainly outdid themselves.

He watched her expectantly. "They don't usually have this on the room service menu. It took a little persuasion to have it all sent up at once."

"You didn't have to go through all the trouble." She eyed it speculatively before looking at him again.

"Why not? We're here, we might as well enjoy what the resort has to offer."

"Where should we start?" Her gaze swept undecidedly over the spread.

"How about the caviar?" He pointed at the little puffs bearing the tiny black beads.

"Why not?" Jackie took one and nibbled it delicately as she watched him.

He took the tiny morsel in one bite and chewed thoughtfully. Logan caught Jackie's amused gaze. "What?"

"Just watching you eat caviar like it's nothing. Just seems so strange."

He swallowed and sighed. "Considering where I came from?"

She looked as if she girded herself for another argument as she replied, "Considering you hate fish."

"Things change." He reached for another and popped it into his mouth to prove his point.

The sparkle in her eyes waned a little. "They certainly do."

Logan carefully laid out all the dishes on the fabric and weighed what he would say next. He didn't want to push her to tears, definitely didn't want to make her relive anything that would upset her, but he needed to know what had happened to make their relationship implode.

"You seem to have a lot on your mind."

She did too. Instead of diving into the incredibly artistic and delicious smelling food, Jackie watched him with great interest.

"I'm not going to bite your head off, you know."

Jackie's eyes widened slightly and her gaze immediately dropped away. She attempted to cover her surprise by picking up a scallop and taking a bite. At least she thought she did. Logan caught her unease.

"This is delicious. You have to try it." She held it out to show him what she'd picked up.

Logan did as he was told and closed his lips over the morsel in her fingers. He slowly retreated, running his tongue over her sauce-covered fingers as he did so.

The reticence in her eyes immediately burned away in a flash of desire.

"You're right. It's fantastic."

Jackie mumbled something and reached for another, only to pick up the drink that waited next to the plate. She took a sip and sighed with delight.

"I take it they did well with the pairings."

She took another less careful sip. "It's wonderful. Like they knew exactly what drink would allow you to taste even the tiniest nuance of the food."

Jackie put the tiny half empty glass aside and went back for the caviar and its complementing wine. This time she gave an appreciative groan. "This is even better."

It was bad enough watching her eat with her fingers, licking and sucking on them, but Logan was getting harder listening to her contented exclamations. If he closed his eyes she could almost imagine her sucking him and making the same noises.

"Aren't you going to have anything else?" Jackie blinked at him innocently.

Was she playing with him?

Logan picked up the foie gras and held it out for her to take a bite before he took the rest. It was rich. Delicious. It put a smile on his face. But not because of how good it was. He had never even heard of foie gras before Jackie had come into his life. It wasn't until she'd spoken of the foods her family liked to dine on or the places they had traveled or even their possessions that he'd realized that there was an entire world that he could never access.

At least not until he'd made enough money.

Once he had, it was almost magical the way the right amount of cash would open even the tightest locked doors.

It had taken him a little while to learn that opening every door wasn't the boon that he thought it would be. Or that every woman would be like Jackie.

He steered his mind away from *those* thoughts in favor of watching Jackie eat once again. Discomfort in his pants was preferable to the memory of women who hadn't given a shit about him but only about the number in his bank account.

It certainly had been a learning curve.

Speaking of curves…

Jackie had leaned over to take a sniff of the red snapper and the front of her dress gaped, giving him quite a tantalizing view.

"If you don't want me to drown in my own drool, you should probably sit back."

She looked down and immediately dropped back onto her butt with a dull thud. He choked on his next breath watching as the move also caused her skirt to flutter, giving him a glimpse of her pussy before it settled on her thighs once again.

"Better?"

Not even remotely. Logan nodded but grabbed the closest glass and pounded it in one go. It did nothing to relieve the ache in his groin or to allay the urge to drag her under him and get back inside her as soon as possible.

Jackie observed him with open curiosity, but said nothing as she continued to sample bits of every dish. Her vocalization of her appreciation each time sent more and more blood to his cock until he was so hard it was almost painful. Logan watched her pluck food with her delicate fingers and slip them into her mouth, practically purring with delight, making it increasingly hard trying to come up with reasons not to jump her.

She reached for another glass, the one paired with the snapper this time. As she did, the strap of her dress slipped off her shoulder, dragging the fabric dangerously low until the hard peak of her nipple was the only thing keeping it up.

As he reached for another glass, he caught her gaze and the tiny smile playing on her lips. It was intentional! Jackie knew exactly what she was doing!

Grumbling, he gripped her arm and dragged her over to him. "I can't believe you'd let me swallow my tongue just to get your kicks."

Jackie laughed and she fell against Logan's broad chest. It had started as an accident. She was becoming anxious when she could see he wanted to talk about something. Only she hadn't wanted to find out what about. When she'd realized what effect the noises she made had on him, the naughty side of her had emerged, wanting to see just how far she could push him. While at the same time distracting him from conversation.

Two birds killed with one very pleasurable stone.

She watched as Logan picked up the incredibly decadent looking dessert.

"What do you think you're going to do with that?" Jackie tried to edge away but he held her tight.

He smiled. "Will you relax?"

Logan swiped his finger through the rich Chantilly cream and held it out between them, presumably for her to taste.

Jackie leaned forward to lick a little off his finger, but he surged forward and did the same. They met in the middle covered in the sweet mixture. Their tongues tangled, allowing her to taste the mingled essences of the cream and Logan before he came in for a devastatingly hot kiss. The result was indescribably delicious, addictive and blasted arousal through her to settle low in her belly and between her thighs. If only she could get this every day…

She forced herself to stop thinking along those lines.

This was here and now — a distraction — and nothing more.

"What's wrong?"

When she drew back, the quizzical expression was clear on Logan's face.

She pinched a large chunk of the cake and stuffed it in his mouth. "Nothing at all."

His beautiful eyes narrowed. He knew he'd been challenged. Wasting no time, he hauled her close and lowered his lips to hers, sharing the cake.

The mix of decadent chocolate and sinfully delicious Logan was heady, and it didn't take long for her head to reel from the sheer power of his kiss.

Logan tugged at her dress strap. "I know I promised nothing would happen, but you started it. So, I'm going to ask. Do you want this?"

"Yes."

He grinned. "Then let's lose the dress."

Jackie leaned forward, helping him slip it up and over her head. He tossed it over his shoulder.

"I'm feeling artistic." Logan eased her back. "Indulge me?"

When he picked up the cake, she grinned. "Go for it."

Logan circled his finger slowly in the cream and dragged it over her lips and down her chin until it petered out on her throat. He repeated the action, continuing the line down her chest between her breasts.

Jackie closed her eyes, letting him do as he liked, enjoying the dueling sensations of the heat of his finger versus the chill of the cream. She felt him tracing patterns over her skin. Spirals around her breasts that circled tighter and tighter around her nipple. He topped them with cool dollops of cream that only made them harden further.

He swept his fingers over her abdomen, painting her skin. Then down her legs.

Then, for a long moment, there was nothing. What was he doing? She was about to open her eyes to find out, but he closed his mouth over her nipple. Logan licked her clean using long strokes of his tongue. He alternated the lashes with gentle suction before moving to the other and giving it the same excruciatingly slow treatment.

Arching under him, she sighed when he drew his tongue over her abdomen then down one leg and up the other, staying well away from where she wanted him most.

"Logan..."

He edged his way up her leg, slowing his movements even more. Drawing out the torture.

Jackie clawed her hands in his hair, doing what she could to drag him closer to where she wanted him.

Chuckling, he relented. Logan let Jackie guide him between her thighs and finally pressed his lips against her folds.

Sparks of pleasure radiated from his touch, causing her to involuntarily arch against his mouth. It gave him the perfect angle to slide his tongue deeper. Logan bobbed his head, thrusting his tongue into her, curling it around her clit on the way out.

Jackie held him tightly when he sucked on clit and gently licked her, building the pleasure until the pressure reached the point of explosion. She tried to stifle the cry, but the wave of sensation was just too great to contain. She trembled in orgasm with a gasping cry of, "Logan!"

He slid up her body and took the cry into his mouth as he adjusted himself and drove his cock deeply into her.

Logan ended the kiss just as her lungs began to burn for air and stared into her eyes as he thrust. Each rock of his hips plunged his thick erection inside her, reaching that spot deep inside that drove her crazy. When he found it, he changed the motion of his hips, holding her gaze as he circled them, swirling the head of his cock into her sensitive nerve endings.

Jackie didn't think he could make her feel any better, but was so glad she had been wrong. Nothing about sex with Logan was ever soft, quiet or tame. She never wanted it to be. He just seemed to know exactly what she was in the mood for and how to give it to her.

She arched into him, wanting him to feel the same ecstasy she was.

Logan grinned at her as he lengthened his thrusts, changing the angle once again so that the wide head of his erection dragged on the roof of her pussy on the way out.

Her jaw dropped and her lungs hitched at the sensation.

"I know," he groaned. "You feel amazing."

Jackie couldn't speak — only feel. Her orgasm hovered so close. Toes curled from the pleasure, she gripped his hips and tried to get him to focus his movements.

Logan took the hint. His hands tight on her hips, Logan held Jackie in place as he drove into her. His gaze stayed locked on hers as he worked them both toward stunning orgasms.

Jackie let her eyes drift closed as she spiraled toward climax, intending on savoring every sensation.

"Keep your eyes open. I want to see you come."

She did and the moment their eyes met, it hit her without warning like a tidal wave.

Jackie dug her nails into his back as if he was the only thing keeping her from oblivion, but kept her eyes open and focused on his.

She watched as Logan joined her, his face contorting in pleasure so extreme it almost looked painful.

They lay there for a time floating in the blissful afterglow.

Logan rolled to his side as he caught his breath. "I must be crushing you."

The thing was, Jackie didn't really mind. She enjoyed the feel of his weight on her. Smiling, she shook her head. "Not really."

Still, he tipped to the side, careful not to crush her. "Shall we hit the shower?"

"In a bit." She felt too deliciously languid to attempt movement just yet. Jackie stretched a little and let her eyes drift close.

"You know, I used to dream about taking us to places like this simply so we could be naked the whole time."

That snapped her out of her blissful state. It seemed her tactic hadn't worked after all. She regretted not taking that shower now.

"Yeah?" Jackie shifted, trying to think of the best next move. Finally, she rolled over to look at him.

Logan shoved his arm under his head to improve his view of her. "What?"

"Can we stick to the deal not to talk about anything other than the here and now?"

He lowered his eyebrows as he turned to face her as well. "Why? I think we've moved past that now."

Jackie couldn't stop the scowl from dragging her mouth downward. "Why, because we've had sex?"

He returned her expression with a wry smirk. "More than just sex, Jackie, and you know it."

"It's been what it's always been like between us." That, at least, was the truth.

Logan gripped one of her hands between his. "It's as though nothing has changed."

Jackie bit her lip as she drew her hand away. "Exactly."

Biting back a snarl, he pulled away and began searching for his clothes. Why was she being so infuriating? Why wouldn't she talk to him just a little?

He stepped into his trousers and threw on his shirt.

Why did he care? This was supposed to be about sex. Simple. But would it hurt her to just admit that when they had sex it was extraordinary? That it meant more?

He gritted his teeth and jammed his feet into his shoes.

What truly aggravated him was that she sat there and watched him get dressed without a word. As though she didn't care whether he left or not.

Maybe she didn't?

The thought that she couldn't care less that he was angry and leaving incensed him further.

"Jackie."

She hesitated but finally met his gaze.

"What are you keeping from me?"

She just stared at him and shook her head. What made it worse was the anguish in them as she told him, "Please go, Logan."

What choice did he have but to leave?

Logan glared at her before striding out and slamming the door behind him with a resounding bang.

Chapter Eight

Jackie stared at the darkening sky from the sun lounger on her deck. Logan was long gone and she wasn't sure if she'd be seeing him again after his angry departure.

He hadn't changed in that respect. Still bullheaded and determined to get what he wanted. Obviously, her feelings or thoughts on the matter didn't figure into the equation.

He had simply grabbed his clothes, slung them on and stormed out. Very much the Logan she remembered.

The clouds were still darker than the sky and patched it in wispy streaks, creating fanciful shapes. A few stars pricked through the inkiness to twinkle faintly.

Taking a long breath, she inhaled the fresh air and just let her limbs hang loosely. For the first time since she arrived, she felt calm considering what she was dealing with.

She didn't want to talk about the past. What had happened, had. Nothing they could say now would change that. Why couldn't he let it go and just let them enjoy themselves?

Because his goals had changed.

As far as she could tell, he wanted to take things further and wanted to make amends for the past. There wasn't much he could do to make things up to her. And getting back together with him was out of the question. They had a good time in bed and out, but when things took a serious turn… That's when it all fell apart.

She didn't want to go through that again.

Jackie couldn't.

It was probably best if she ended things now. But she was so weak when it came to Logan. Hadn't their time together proven that? He was like an addiction she didn't want to quit.

Perhaps it was time to throw herself into her bridesmaid duties.

It made sense, after all that's what she was there for. She needed to be a better friend to Caroline.

With that plan in place in her head, Jackie settled back in her seat.

Now for the follow-through.

* * * *

Logan paced his room, though it did nothing to alleviate the frustration and anger coursing through him.

He wasn't going to get anywhere with Jackie stonewalling him. He doubted he'd get anything from Caroline.

But Charles…

Couples getting married talked, didn't they? Caroline might have talked about Jackie.

Logan sighed. Was he really going to go and interrogate a man he barely knew on the eve of his wedding? It was crazy.

But he was grasping at straws. He would have to use a little stealth and a lot of charm if he was going to get anything out of Charles and not come across like a crazed stalker.

But why wouldn't Jackie talk to him about what happened? Had he done something wrong? Had she? If she had, what would be so bad as to warrant her wanting to end things? The worst thing in his mind was cheating. But Jackie wouldn't have cheated on him any more than he would have on her. While they had been together, all others had been eclipsed by Jackie and Logan wanted to believe it had been the same for her.

So what had happened? Her parents? Her father had certainly taken enough joy in telling him that Jackie didn't want anything to do with him ever again.

Had that been the truth? Logan was beginning to distrust his own memories. The way Jackie was behaving definitely shrouded what he'd thought had happened in doubt. She hurt, and that gnawed at his gut.

It was time to find out the truth.

* * * *

The sun painted the outside world gold as Logan headed to the restaurant where he knew everyone congregated for breakfast. So far, he hadn't joined them simply because he didn't really know anyone and didn't feel too inclined to change that fact.

But if he wanted information, he had to make nice with them.

Even if it made him feel like a fraud.

When he loped in, he was greeted by curious gazes, which he ignored. Logan made his way to the table filled with groomsmen and took a seat. Luckily, it was across from Charles.

"Morning."

They accepted his gruff greeting with amusement. Charles in particular grinned.

"Had a rough night?"

Did he look that bad? It wasn't surprising, considering he hadn't gotten any sleep. He grunted something that the others took as 'Why, yes. I had woman trouble' because they all shuffled closer with expressions of curiosity and commiseration on their faces.

"Have some juice." Charles pushed a drink toward him that smelled suspiciously like it contained more vodka than orange juice.

He took it anyway. "Thanks."

Doug nudged him. "So what happened? Was it something to do with your hot ex? You know, she's so prim and proper, I bet she's a wildcat between the sheets."

The fact that the man had even considered what Jackie was like in bed made him want to twist his head off, but he shook it off and took a swig of the so-called orange juice.

"I knew it!" Charles declared triumphantly. The rest of the men shared looks of commiseration. "We've all been there."

One of the men, Logan knew him as Phil, grinned lasciviously. "Let me guess. You had a hot night and now she wants more?"

"Not exactly." He wasn't even in the ballpark. If they knew what he and Jackie had been up to their heads would have exploded.

He wasn't going to get anywhere with these idiots around. "Can I talk to you, Charles? Privately?"

There were groans from around the table when a quizzical-looking Charles nodded his assent. "Of course." He grabbed his drink and led the way to a secluded table well away from prying eyes.

They slid into opposing seats. For a long moment, they just stared at each other while Logan tried to formulate the questions in a way that didn't make him come across as Crazy Stalker Ex.

"So… What's up?" Charles paled a little. "You're not going to back out of the wedding over your ex, are you? I can swap you with another woman if you need."

Logan shook his head. "It's nothing like that." At least not yet.

"So?"

"I wanted to know if Caroline said anything to you about me and Jackie in the past."

Charles frowned. "Not really. After the shock reunion the other day, she said you two had a past and that was about it. Then she read me the riot act for not telling her I recruited you and blah, blah, blah."

Logan didn't have the patience to listening to his blathering. "Nothing about why we broke up before?"

Charles lowered his pale eyebrows until they met in a confused furrow. "No. Should she have?"

Logan shook his head.

"Look, if you two hooked up and it's getting a bit messy, just let her know who's the boss and that if it's not going to happen, that's all there is to it."

Logan sat there letting it sink in and it dawned on him that not only had Charles gotten it completely backward, he had as well. Jackie was the one who didn't want to take anything further. So what did that make him? The woman in their relationship? What Charles said did make sense, though, and it had been what she had told him.

Jackie drew the line and expected him to be a grown up about it and respect that. And what had he done?

Been an asshole.

He downed the rest of the drink. "Thanks for that. I've got to run."

Charles looked at him quizzically. "Don't you ever eat?"

"When I have time." He got up and nodded his goodbye.

"We've got the rehearsal dinner tonight. You'll show up for that at least, right?"

Logan barely heard him. "Yeah. No problem."

He hastily jogged along the halls and pathways until he found himself in front of Jackie's door. How to commence groveling without actually looking like he was begging for forgiveness?

He knocked and waited.

Would Jackie even answer?

He waited a moment longer, but when there was no answer, fear fluttered in his chest. Would she have left? He doubted Jackie would let Caroline down like that. Much like himself, Jackie did seem to prefer hiding out in her room to joining in with the others. So if she wasn't there, where was she?

He vaguely wondered if he would find her in the spa once again. Blood rushed to his cock at the thought of repeating their last visit. Perhaps they could find something new to do there.

Logan pulled out his phone and, with no qualms, accessed the hotel security cameras with a few flicks and a secure login. There was some advantage to running the security to the hotel. He knew he was skirting a fine line with what he was doing, and that Jackie would probably be horrified if she found out what he was doing. But it wasn't like he was invading anyone's privacy, he only took a look at the feeds from the cameras in the common areas, after all. It gave him enough to track her out onto the beach.

He logged out and followed the path Jackie had taken out into the sunshine. It wasn't long before he found her.

She wore the same one piece suit from before, but had covered up her delicious ass with a sarong. A detail he was glad for. There was a primitive part of his brain that didn't want anyone else seeing her.

It was ridiculous since she wasn't with him. He didn't own her. But the thought of any other man getting a glimpse of her ass — or any other part of her for that matter — drove him nuts.

Logan took a slow breath as he approached. "Hey, Jackie."

She started and turned to face him. Even though he couldn't see her eyes behind the dark sunglasses, he could tell she was on guard from her stance. Her shoulders were tight, her jaw obstinate. Jackie looked like she was ready to punch him if she had to.

That was new.

Jackie was the gentlest person he'd ever known. For her to want to strike out was the ultimate in her last lines of defense.

The realization that she was so on guard made him sick to his stomach. He slowed and put up his hands. "I just want to talk. And to apologize for my behavior last night."

Jackie's posture relaxed somewhat, but he doubted he had her convinced.

He took a step closer. "I just wanted you to know that you're in the driver's seat. I'm just along for the ride. I realize that I've been acting like a total asshole. All I've been caring about is what I wanted. I should have paid more attention to your wants and needs."

"Yeah, you should have."

At least she was speaking to him. He took a breath and carried on. "I'm not going to say that I don't have questions. What we have between us is rare. And you and I both know it. But something happened between us years ago, and I want to know what it was that drove us apart."

Jackie inhaled to rebut, but he shook his head. "I won't force you to answer. If you never do, I'll just have to live with it. I just want to spend time with you. And when our time's up and you want to end it... I won't be happy, but I'll accept it."

Jackie stared at him. He was saying all the right things. But could she believe him? Why should she?

To be truthful, he might have been a jerk about things, but she knew what his temper was like. And his focus. When Logan Forrester wanted something, he would do whatever it took to get it.

But she also knew he was a man of his word. If he said he would drop it, he would, even if it killed him.

"I would like to spend time together." She stepped closer and studied his eyes, though she wasn't sure what she was searching for. "I do agree with you that what we have is something unique. But I'm not about to forget about everything else just to have it for a short while. We're here for our friends' wedding. That should be our priority."

"You're right. Though they're more your friends than mine. I'm just involved because they were short a man." He shrugged. "I was reminded that we have the rehearsal dinner tonight? When's the practice wedding scheduled to happen?"

"Tomorrow morning. At ten." And not a moment later—Caroline had a schedule that nothing short of an act of God would change.

"Wonderful." He sounded anything but thrilled.

Jackie wasn't sure what to say next. In lieu of standing and staring at him dumbly, she started walking. She knew he would fall in step beside her, and he did. They ambled for a while and they made it to the waterline before she looked at him again.

Logan's brow was furrowed and his jaw rigid. He stared stonily at the water, as if it could answer his questions if he intimidated it enough.

Logan was a handsome man. Tall, broad shouldered, classical features. He could have been a sculpture. The breeze riffled his hair and softly wafted his scent to her. It was like everything about him was engineered to derail her brain and whip her hormones into a frenzy.

He must have felt her gaze on him because he turned his beautiful eyes to her. "What?"

"Nothing." She sighed. "So when you say spend time together, what exactly do you mean? Like, as a couple?"

"If that's what you want. If you want to keep it light, I'm good with that too. Like I said, I just want to spend time with you to get to know you again."

That sounded both wonderful and pointless. "What good would it do, Logan? We'd just get attached to one another again and..."

"And what?" he challenged.

It would be more excruciating than the last time they had to part ways? "It might not be the smartest idea."

Logan wrapped his arms around her. "I never claimed to be a smart man."

Jackie couldn't deny that she enjoyed the sensation of him cocooned around her. She felt warm. Protected. Safe.

Jackie chuckled into his chest. "Neither am I, it seems."

"What I want is another chance. We were good together once. We still are in a lot of ways. I just want to find out if we can go the distance this time around."

She stared up at him, straight in the eyes. "Okay." With a trial period so short, nothing could really develop between them. It would at least leave her heart intact this time.

Logan shifted to hold her from behind like he always used to. Arms secure around her shoulders and his chin light on the top of her head. She could almost imagine that they were the same kids who believed they would be together forever and happily ride off into the sunset.

They stayed that way for a long time simply staring at the surf. If Jackie hadn't known better she would have thought he was trying to learn what she wanted through osmosis.

Logan pressed his nose against her hair and sighed. "So what do you want to do until we have to grace them with our presence at the dinner?"

"What else is there to do?"

"There's an aquarium." He lowered his head to whisper in her ear. "Or we could go to the spa again. There are many rooms there we haven't violated yet."

Heat blossomed, unfurling low in her belly to envelop her body. That certainly had its possibilities. "Why don't you set that up while we check out the aquarium?"

Logan grinned. "You got it."

Jackie had wondered where they could possibly put an aquarium in the hotel. Logan led the way with a secretive smile on his face the entire time. He knew how much she loved the ocean and seeing the creatures living there. There was just something so soothing about the blue of the water and watching the animals swim. If she could have, Jackie would spend all her time in the ocean.

Logan followed a path that led them deeper into the hotel and, at the same time, the mountain.

Confused, Jackie looked at him. "Did we take a wrong turn somewhere?"

Logan chuckled and shook his head. "Nope. Just keep walking."

What choice did she have when he had her pinned to his side and he continued?

Jackie got the impression that not only were they going farther into the bedrock, but they were also descending. Yet somehow the lighting stayed bright and natural and the air fresh. She didn't know how they did it, but it was incredible.

But her breath caught when they reached what could only be their destination.

The lighting had dimmed, giving the cavern-like space a mysterious blue glow. The only way she could figure the engineers did it was they cut off the side of the mountain and replaced it with an immense pane of glass. It gave them an unprecedented glimpse into the world outside.

Fingers of light filtered through the water to act almost like a spotlight on the brilliantly colored fish and coral. It was the next best thing to actually being out there in the water.

Mesmerized, Jackie walked up to the glass and pressed her palms against the cool barrier between them and the ocean. "This is the most incredible thing I've ever seen."

He came up behind her and closed his large hands around her hips. "I thought you would like it."

"I love it."

He dragged her back to one of the benches set up for visitors to relax and enjoy the view.

Jackie sat and leaned against Logan as she watched the fish swim past. They darted in and out of the rainbow-colored coral scattering other fish, winding around others. A turtle lazily glided through while in the distance she was sure she caught the ominous silhouette of a shark.

"I could spend all day here."

She felt rather than heard his chuckle. "I know. It's a good thing I planned a little bit ahead on this one since I knew you couldn't resist." Logan looked toward the door. "You can bring it in."

Jackie turned to watch as a waiter from the restaurant walked in carrying a covered tray and a colorful blanket. With a broad smile, he one-handedly spread the blanket over one of the other benches and placed the tray upon it before discreetly exiting.

"So this was all planned, was it?" Jackie let Logan help her to her feet and walked over to the other bench. They settled on either end with the tray in the middle.

Logan shrugged. "Maybe. Don't tell me you don't love a well-organized man."

He knew she did, especially when things were planned out and went without a hitch.

"So what's under there?" Jackie anticipated another succulent meal so when he lifted the lid she burst out laughing.

Underneath were two tropical-looking drinks, complete with umbrellas. Skewered pineapple chunks piled high on a plate quickly filled the air with their scent. The thing that made her laugh, however, was the pair of binoculars resting next to them.

"You've thought of everything," Jackie picked up the binoculars and turned to look at the water, though she figured they were more for comedic effect than anything else.

"Just call me Mr. Boy Scout."

The last thing she equated Logan with was a Boy Scout. She put the binoculars down, and he handed her a drink.

She held up the drink and appraised the layers that graduated from the deep red at the bottom to bubblegum pink at the top. "What's in this?"

He smirked. "I'm not trying to get you drunk if that's what you're thinking. It's mostly fruit juice with a hint of rum."

Jackie took a delicate sip and let the exotic blend of flavors burst on her tongue. She groaned with delight. "This is fantastic."

Logan was mid-sip and nodded in agreement as he swallowed. "Very good."

The drink was replaced by a skewer, and Jackie took a juicy bite of the pineapple. Like the drink, the fruit was out of this world.

Jackie groaned. "You have to try this." She held her skewer for him to take a bite.

Logan looked a little pained as he did. That was when she remembered what her exclamations over the food the night before had done to him.

Biting her lip, she contemplated how to put that information to good use as he took a slurping bite of the pineapple.

Jackie dropped the fruit, cupped his cheeks and pulled him in for a kiss. His lips were still coated with the sweet juice of the pineapple, and she darted her tongue out to taste. Running it over his lower lip, she moaned her delight at the flavor of Logan and pineapple.

He took the kiss further, parting her lips. She accepted his tongue and the fruit juice along with it. She enjoyed the tease and the taste for a long moment before she was gasping for air.

Reluctantly, Logan pulled back.

For an instant, Jackie wondered if it was because of where they were. But since when had they shied away from getting physical in public?

Logan took the tray and put it on the floor. "The last thing we need is to break something and let people know what we're doing in here."

She blinked at him innocently. "And just what would that be?"

He tugged her close and nipped her shoulder. "Whatever you want."

She tilted her head to look at him. "And if I wanted to just sit here and stare at the water?"

"Doable."

Jackie smiled. "Then let's do that for a little while."

Logan handed Jackie her drink then picked up his own before snaking an arm over her shoulders. It was just so comfortable. He couldn't think of another time in recent history that he'd felt so relaxed. And to be spending time with Jackie doing nothing but absorbing the ambience might have sounded boring, but it was doing miracles for him.

Jackie was like a balm to his soul.

Everything just felt right. So why was he convinced that it wasn't going to last?

He knew he shouldn't let the past make any difference to what they had now. They were different people, and grownups at that. The last time they had been together, they had been nothing but wide-eyed kids. Perhaps that was the reason things went wrong.

They only had a few days left and he knew it was hardly enough time to reinvigorate their relationship. He got the feeling that Jackie liked that fact more than she was letting on.

It was insane, for sure, to think that in less than a week anything would change between them. But it was a start. The more time he spent with Jackie the more he wanted. And it wasn't just the lust talking. He wasn't the type to go jumping through hoops for just anyone.

It just turned out that the only one who had hoops he was even slightly interested in navigating was Jackie.

Jackie Pennington was the one.

Now to convince Jackie he was the one for her.

That might be a bit harder and take much longer. Logan would bide his time. Now that he'd found her again he would do whatever it took, no matter how long, to get her to love him again.

And if he told her any of this she would probably laugh in his face. He might not have been the most demonstrative guy before, and maybe that had been part of what went wrong, but he could start.

Giving her attention, physical and otherwise, was no hardship, especially now when he had more time to spend on her.

That reminded him, he needed to sort out that spa trip.

Grinning, he pulled out his phone and texted the spa exactly what he wanted.

It would definitely be unforgettable.

He also took the moment to covertly disable the cameras pointed at them.

"Remembered about the spa?"

She looked up at him with a knowing smile.

"Yeah. Just making sure we're booked in."

She took a sip sighing again. "So what have you got us in for?"

"You're just going to have to wait and see."

Jackie giggled. Maybe the tiny bit of rum in the drink was going to her head.

"Will it be anything like our last visit?"

That took him off guard. The rum was definitely making its effect known. "I did have something along those lines in mind, but only if you're up for it."

"Really now?" Jackie stretched against him and nipped his earlobe as she whispered, "Have anything in mind for right now?"

Hell, yes. When didn't he? Since they'd met up again, every time they were together it was like a waking wet dream. One thing that he loved about her was the fact that she was up for just about anything. She trusted him. Even though they took risks, she was right about him doing whatever it took to keep her safe and away from prying eyes. He loved that she wasn't afraid to show him that side of herself.

Even now, she lightly traced lines up his thigh toward his rapidly growing erection.

"I'm thinking you have a few thoughts on the matter?"

Logan mimicked her moves, but reached his goal much quicker. Thank goodness for the bathing suit she wore. He slipped his hand under her sarong and traced the hem of her suit.

Logan insinuated his fingers between her legs and under the stretchy fabric.

"No fair. I can't get under your jeans as easily."

"This was your idea. Maybe you should have planned it out better," he teased.

Circling her clit, he grinned when she gasped. She wouldn't take any offense from the comment.

"Let me in."

She parted her thighs farther, allowing him whatever access he wanted.

"Just for the record…" She groaned when he plunged his fingers into her. "I wanted this to be mutual."

Chuckling, he pumped his fingers, making sure to graze her clit with the heel of his hand with each inward thrust.

He grazed her shoulder with his teeth, making his way slowly up to her ear to whisper, "I want to feel you come around my fingers."

Logan felt the tremor ripple through her at his words. Jackie was getting close. He loved that she was so responsive to him.

Taking a furtive glance at the entrance of the room, he upped the power and tempo of his thrusts until he felt her shudder and she clamped around his fingers. Logan caught her cry of ecstasy with his free hand as he continued to coax out every last shudder of her orgasm and she leaned, limp and pliant, against him.

He wrapped his arms around her until her trembling subsided. "I hope that was a good appetizer."

Jackie let out a breathy laugh. "It was so good I don't think I can handle the rest of the meal just yet."

That made him laugh. "How about we get out of here?"

"Can we at least wait until I can stand without falling over?"

"Of course." Logan grabbed the tray and tidied up a little while he waited. "Though I could carry you."

That made her laugh. He loved the sound of it as it echoed around the room. It also reminded him that he needed to get the cameras back online before anyone noticed.

Whipping out his phone, he then deftly took care of it in seconds before he shoved it back in his pocket and carried on. Once he had the tray sorted he held his hand out to her. Jackie took it with a weary smile and grabbed the blanket with her free hand.

"Instead of the spa, mind if we just lazed about on the beach until dinner?"

It would give him time to hone his idea for their time at the spa. "Sure. I just need to change and let the spa know."

The spa was easily taken care of with a quick text as they walked. They quickly reached his suite, even with the long, meandering path they followed.

Logan swiped his card and, seconds later, they were in his suite. The cleaning staff had been through and tidied. The room was spotless and even had new flowers in all the vases lending the room their wonderful scent. As he placed the tray down on the table, Jackie buried her nose in one of the arrangements. He had no idea what the flowers were but they were pretty, and were brightly colored befitting the ambience.

He quickly dug through his luggage and grabbed his trunks and a bottle of sunscreen. "Make yourself at home. I'm just going to get changed."

"Okay." She picked up the dome from the tray, pinched a chunk of pineapple off a stick then sucked it between her lips.

Biting back a groan, he headed into the bathroom.

Logan considered taking a cold shower, but it wouldn't do him any good. Whenever he was around Jackie he was a walking hard-on.

He changed and slathered himself with sunscreen, ready for some time in the baking sun.

After a good long stare at himself in the mirror and a few breaths, he walked back out to find the room empty.

Had she left?

"Jackie?"

"Over here."

Her voice came from the other side of the suite, from the pool.

He found Jackie with her sarong off and her curvy body stretched out on one of his loungers. He wasn't going to complain. Logan slid onto the other.

"I guess we're staying here, then?"

Jackie opened up one eye to look at him. "It's better than getting gritty with sand."

Arranging himself on the lounger, he sighed. "I definitely agree." And this way they didn't have to rush around before having to go down to dinner. Well, he didn't. Jackie would still need to go to her suite, but he definitely preferred staying inside than going out.

Turning his head, he studied Jackie, who looked as though she'd already fallen asleep. Her dark lashes dusted her cheeks, and her chest rose and fell slowly and rhythmically. He wouldn't be surprised if she napped after the drink and the orgasm.

Thankfully, the sunlight wasn't directly on the deck. So that was a blessing. But it was still bright enough to warm the skin. Maybe once she woke up, he could convince her to take a dip with him in the pool.

"I know you think I'm sleeping." She smiled though didn't open her eyes. "I'm just very relaxed."

"Glad to hear it."

Logan did the best he could to reach the same Zen state that Jackie had found. Only he couldn't make himself comfortable on the chair. It wasn't because of the chair itself. Logan knew it was him. He was restless, but wasn't quite sure how he would assuage it.

He wasn't even sure why he was so twitchy. Jackie seemed to be content with what they were doing. He certainly was. Logan just wanted more.

Only there was a giant invisible wall dividing them. It bothered him that he didn't know what it was made of, which left him incapable of navigating it. And not knowing how to deal with something was intolerable. He'd made a career out of finding ways of fixing problems and here was one staring him in the face that he had no clue how to deal with. And of course it had to be more important to him than any job he'd ever had.

His usual mode of operation was to dissect the problem and look at it from every angle to see what he could discern from the bits. Other than picking apart Jackie's brain, Logan was short of options. He could go back and try Charles again, though he doubted he knew anything that was going on. Caroline would hardly want to talk to him about anything, least of all Jackie.

The rest of the family there would be a crap shoot. Would they even be worth the effort? They had a finite amount of time together. Did he really want to waste it on other people? Gaining her trust and talking things out would be the sanest route but wouldn't meet his need for instant gratification.

Sighing, he dropped his head back against the seat and closed his eyes. He would bide his time. Let things unfurl at their own pace. Logan clenched his hands into fists before forcing them to relax and fall to his sides.

"Is something wrong?

He looked over to see Jackie watching him with a strange expression on her face.

"Fine. Just tired. Have a lot of things on my mind."

Jackie twisted to her side to face him. "Nothing bad, I hope."

"Just work stuff."

"Tell me about it."

He mirrored her pose. This seemed promising. "That wasn't part of the rules, was it?"

Color lit up her cheeks. "Right. I forgot."

Was she going to let it drop? He could very easily do the same, but Logan decided to use it to make a show of good faith.

"You asked, so you obviously want to know." He put up his hand when she started to protest. "I don't want you to think that because I'm telling you things that you have to do the same. It's totally up to you." But he hoped that she would share a little about herself.

"Anyway, I'm a security software designer. My software runs the security for this hotel and many others."

Her eyes widened, but she smiled warmly. "That's amazing! Congratulations. You've always wanted to make it big and you have."

"Thanks." The pride he felt from her acknowledgment of his achievements was immense.

Logan watched her closely and for a long moment she seemed conflicted. There was something she wanted to say, but after a silent war with herself she stayed quiet.

He couldn't say he wasn't disappointed. Why didn't she feel that she could open up to him over something as trivial as their jobs? Unless she didn't have one. Her family was wealthy enough for her, her kids and grandkids to never have to lift a finger.

Was she embarrassed about that? Not wanting to make her any more uncomfortable, Logan decided against pushing the subject.

"How's Caroline taking the whole impending nuptials thing?"

"Honestly?" Jackie pressed her lips into a thin line. "You can't tell Charles any of this."

She was going to trust him with a confidence? "Of course not."

"She's a bit jittery. I think it's just a case of cold feet. But she seemed pretty terrified the last time I talked to her about it."

Logan frowned. "What do you think? Is it just nerves or something more? You know her better than anyone else."

The expression that came over Jackie's face was a strange one. She looked almost…sad? That set off a whole new round of questions. Had the same thing happened to her? He pushed that image to the back of his mind. The last thing he needed to think about was Jackie even entertaining the idea of marrying someone else.

Jackie sighed. Maybe once, she had known Caroline better than anyone else, but now that they were simply friends who kept in touch over long distance and met up once in a while… She suspected that she had only been asked to be a bridesmaid as a gesture. They had been close when they were younger and their parents were probably still friends now. It had still been nice to be asked.

To answer his question, she shrugged. "Who knows what goes through a woman's mind just before she gets married?"

Logan's shoulders seemed to relax when she said it. "You've never had the pleasure then?"

She toyed with the idea of staying quiet, but they were getting along so well. Answering a question here and there couldn't hurt. "No."

He seemed satisfied with that. At least for now. "Do you think she'll make it to the altar at least?"

"I hope so, but only if she's ready. I can't imagine how horrible it would be for her to go through with it and realize that she'd made a mistake."

Her phone buzzed just then, and Jackie immediately knew it was going to be Caroline. She turned to Logan. "You know how when you say a person's name a whole bunch of times and they suddenly call or show up?" She held up her phone with an ironic smile before checking her message.

Logan rolled his eyes. "What's she got to say?"

"She wanted to spend some time together and wondered where I was." Jackie lowered the phone to her side. "Why do you dislike Caroline so much?"

Logan snorted. "I think she dislikes me more than the other way around. What I don't like is how you always jump when she calls. You always put her before everything else."

Jackie bolted straight in her chair. "I did not."

"It certainly seemed that way. I never felt as though I took precedence in your life."

That hurt. Logan had been the center of her universe for a while. She'd planned her life around his just so they could spend a few more minutes together and here he was saying he didn't feel loved?

It wasn't like he tried too hard. Every chance he'd gotten he was away for work, or a conference, or a class or a project. She understood that he was driven and was proud at all he had accomplished, but she had been left on the sideline a lot of the time. Not once had she complained when he was off trying to fulfill his dreams.

"I wasn't exactly a part of your world either, Logan." She picked up her wrap and wound it around her waist securely. "I should get going. I need to see if Caroline's okay and get ready for dinner."

Logan frowned but he nodded. "I'll see you there."

She slid off he lounger and was about to leave, but she turned to nearly crash into his chest. He was going to walk her out. Jackie sighed. "You don't have to walk me out."

"What kind of gentleman would I be?" His words might have been blithe, but he still looked tense.

Jackie didn't feel much better. What did she want out of this? She knew he was going to push to get what he wanted, but she wasn't sure what that was. Perhaps he did want a relationship? It certainly felt that way. But what if it was just a tactic on his part? A game? She had been hurt by him once before. So badly.

On the other hand, they fit together so well. There hadn't been another man Jackie had met that she meshed with as she did with Logan. The time they were spending together was only cementing that fact in her mind.

It would just be so easy to fall back into a relationship with him. They were older now. Things were definitely different. Could they make a go of it this time and make it work?

It would be so wonderful if they could.

Only they needed to talk. Really talk. Get everything out in the open and figure out where to go from there.

No more games.

Her phone buzzed again.

Only now wasn't the time.

They had a few days. She would make the time to talk to him.

Jackie stopped when she reached the door. She turned to Logan and held his gaze. "We'll sit down and talk. Soon."

His smile was small and a bit grim, but he nodded. "We will."

Chapter Nine

Jackie found Caroline, through a series of texts, waiting for her at the stairs to the secret beach. Her friend looked tiny and washed out in a simple white sun dress, staring forlornly at the greenery.

She seemed to snap out of her trance when she saw Jackie.

"Hey." Caroline put away her phone and stared at her.

"What?" Jackie did her best to keep the guilt from her face.

Her friend crossed her arms. "Where were you this time?"

"Exploring the hotel?" It was true enough. Why was Caroline being so confrontational?

"And Logan wasn't anywhere near you, right?"

"Why would that matter?"

Caroline pointed accusingly. "I knew it! He's gotten to you!"

Jackie scrubbed her hand over her face. "Is that why you called me out here? To chastise me?"

"Actually, no. I was freaking out about the wedding, but when I tried to think about something else to calm down it hit me. Ever since you saw him, you've been elusive. Evasive. You're never in your room. He always seems to be around, lurking like some kind of stalker."

"How can he not? We're at the same hotel. He's always going to be around here somewhere."

She narrowed her beautiful green eyes. "And now you're being defensive."

"How can I not when you're attacking me?" Jackie sighed. "What business is it of yours what I do?"

"Because I care about you and the last time you two got together it was a nightmare for you. Or don't you remember how he'd ruined your life?"

Pinching the bridge of her nose, Jackie squeezed her eyes shut for a moment. "Of course I haven't forgotten. And for your information, we're not together. He actually seems to want to make amends for the past."

"You're joking, right?" Caroline gripped her shoulders and shook her slightly. "You cannot let him back into your life. He's just going to mess it all up again!"

Jackie stared into her friend's wide eyes. She wasn't usually this hysterical, especially not about another person's life. It had to be about her own. "What's this really about, Caroline?"

She glared at her. "I'm concerned about my friend?"

"I know you care about me, but I know you're worrying about a lot right now. I can take care of myself."

Caroline took a few deep breaths. "I'm so sorry. I didn't mean to come down on your so hard. I am worried about you. You know I don't want anyone or anything to hurt you. But I'm also going crazy about the wedding." She turned to grip the railing. "I feel like I'm spiraling. What's worse is I have no idea what the baseline is for normal in this kind of situation. Am I really freaking out? Is it just cold feet? Is it normal to want to run for my life a few days before I'm supposed to get married to the love of my life? Is he even the love of my life?" She leaned forward and banged her head on the metal.

That was a lot to deal with. Jackie dragged Caroline away from the railing and gave her a hug. "I can't pretend I know what you're going through but I can't let you dent the railing. The hotel would come after you for compensation and that's just another headache you can do without."

Caroline let out a sniffling laugh. "I'm glad one of us can joke around."

"That's what I'm here for." Jackie held her a moment longer then slowly eased back. "I'm sure what you're feeling is just jitters. All the anticipation is just at its highest point now."

"I guess."

"Forget about all that. Ignore everything else. There are no guests, no wedding, no reception. What does your heart tell you? Do you still want to be with Charles?"

Caroline closed her eyes and after a moment she opened her eyes. "Yes."

"There's your answer."

A smile slowly crept over her lips. "You're right."

"Of course I am." Jackie felt a small weight lift off her shoulders. It was so simple when dealing with other people's problems, why couldn't she do the same for herself?

Why couldn't she?

Putting aside everything that had happened between herself and Logan would be easy but if she discounted them, could she imagine herself being with him?

Jackie ignored everything but their time together the past week and came to the stomach flipping conclusion.

Yes.

"You look like you just got punched in the stomach." Caroline observed her speculatively.

She felt like she had been.

"You still have feelings for Logan, don't you?"

"I think I do." Saying the words aloud gave them more weight.

"How could you after what he did?"

It didn't make sense to her either. All she knew was that when they weren't holding things back, they were good together. Jackie wanted to find out if once they got things out in the open things would be as she hope they could be.

Caroline huffed. "I understand about the whole first love thing. But if I'm being completely honest, I don't know if I could forgive him. Or trust him again, for that matter."

"I know." Wasn't that what she was struggling with already? "I just want to believe he's not all bad, I guess."

"And if he is and he hurts you all over again?"

That's what she was afraid of. Then again, she wasn't going to get anywhere if she continued to fear the future. Hadn't she already learned that? When she'd been lost and alone she hadn't let fear drag her down. She had pulled herself together and had come out better for it.

Somehow this seemed more daunting than anything else she had faced.

Jackie would take it slowly, like wading into the shallows of the ocean. Take a few steps, get acclimated then venture deeper.

Caroline jabbed her with her elbow. "You don't think he'll hurt you again?"

"I hope not, but if he does, then I'll deal with it. I got over it last time and I can do it again."

"And you'll let me kick his ass this time," Caroline said fiercely.

It made Jackie laugh thinking that tiny Caroline could kick anyone's ass.

Her friend's phone pinged, and she sighed as she read her screen. "Time to get dressed for the rehearsal dinner."

"Right."

They walked back in together and parted ways once inside.

Butterflies pin-wheeled in her stomach as she made her way to her room. It was a big step to bare herself to anyone again. It was going to take a bit to build up the courage.

However, once she was at her room and opened the door, the fluttering eased a little and her heart filled her chest until she thought it would burst.

Hanging with the net over her bed was a garment bag with the discreet logo of Gucci and on her bed beneath sat a shoe box emblazoned with Louboutin.

Jackie plucked a little envelope off the shoe box and pulled out the handwritten note.

Hope you like and will wear tonight – Logan

Her hands trembled slightly when she unzipped the bag. Inside she discovered a floaty, sleeveless, almost sheer, jade-green dress. Prefect for the tropical heat. The V-neck didn't plunge down too far and the skirt would reach her knees. A sash of the same material and color was tied at the waist in a bow. It was simple and tasteful and must have cost him a small fortune. Jackie had seen it in several magazines on the flight over gracing models and celebs. The shoes were matching green sling-backs that would boost her height by at least six inches. It would still leave her a couple inches short of Logan.

She couldn't help the smile on her face. It was so sweet of him. Logan had remembered not only her favorite color but labels as well.

After a rushed shower, she quickly got dressed, relishing the feel of the fine fabric against her skin. It fit perfectly. Jackie twisted back and forth in front of the mirror for a minute, enjoying the swish of the dress, before brushing out her hair and putting on her makeup.

She smoothed lotion over her legs from a container she found in the bathroom. It left her skin feeling silky and smelling like a blend of the exotic flowers found all over the island.

The last thing to go on were the shoes. It had been a long time since she'd worn shoes so high and it took her a few steps to regain her balance.

She glanced at herself in the mirror and Jackie almost did a double take. With her hair out of the ponytail and cascading over her shoulders in shining waves, the gorgeous dress and shoes, she looked like the rich and beautiful Jaqueline Pennington once again.

Is that who he wanted? The pampered girl she used to be?

The euphoria faded. That wasn't who she was any longer. And she didn't want to be as spoiled or naïve again. If he wanted to turn her back into that he was in for a rude awakening.

It dawned on her to change out of the dress, but she just didn't have the time. Jackie grabbed her purse and phone and opened the door.

"You're gorgeous." Logan stood on the other side handsome in a finely cut suit. "I'm so glad you decided to wear the dress."

Jackie nodded. "Thanks. You shouldn't have."

She tried to sidestep him, but he closed a gentle hand around her upper arm.

"What's wrong?"

She tried to shrug out of his grasp. "We don't have time to talk. We're going to be late."

He didn't let go. "A few minutes won't hurt. What did I do wrong now?"

She sighed. He wasn't going to let it go without an explanation. "You bought me this dress and shoes."

"So now me buying you things is a problem?"

Jackie refused to meet his gaze. Somehow, that now she was saying the words, it seemed ridiculous. "It was sweet of you, but you shouldn't spend so much on me."

"I can spend my money however I like. And if that means buying you things I'm certain you'll like, it's my prerogative."

She sighed. "I'm not yours to splurge on, Logan."

His expression turned incredulous. "So now I'm showing ownership by buying you nice things?"

"That's not what I'm saying." Jackie was making a mess of this. "Let's go to dinner before we're missed." She stomped ahead and heard him follow, quickly catching up.

"You can't keep using the wedding as a deflector, Jackie."

She picked up the pace. "I'm not. I'm trying to be a responsible adult who can show up on time."

"Right." He stayed quiet for a little while before he asked. "So what is it then?"

"I'm not the same girl that you remember, okay?"

Logan snagged her hand and dragged her back to him. "That's very clear."

Jackie plucked at the skirt. "So why are you trying to dress me up like her?"

His frown deepened. "Who said I was doing that?"

Jackie swept her hand over herself indicating the clothes. "What do you call this?"

"I was trying to do something nice for you?" He raked his hand through his hair. "I remembered what you used to like and assumed that you still do. It was an attempt to give you something, for once."

Shame burned her cheeks. While they had been together in the past she had been the one to give him things. Buying a textbook for him here, a pair of shoes there. It wasn't like he hadn't reciprocated. Logan had when he could afford it. Had that bothered him all this time?

She bit her lip. "I'm sorry. I'm being ungrateful. Thank you. Really. It's beautiful."

"You're welcome." Logan smiled a little. "Did I at least remember your favorite shade of green?"

"You did. I'm surprised you remembered." Her heart swelled over the fact that he had.

"I can recall a lot."

So could she.

The trip to the hotel restaurant was short. This meal was being held in one of the other restaurants in the hotel. Instead of the huge aquarium in the center of the room, this time the wonder that drew her eyes was the beautiful beach spread like a painting outside. The wall-sized doors were opened so that instead of it being a backdrop, it became part of the dining room. White lights imitated stars on the ceiling and delicately lit the white lily and vivid pink plumeria centerpieces on the tables, giving it all a fairy tale-like atmosphere.

"This is *beautiful*." Jackie took a moment just to stare.

"Yeah, it looks great.

She rolled her eyes when he wouldn't see.

"Jackie!" Caroline appeared out of nowhere in an elegant pink dress that grazed the floor as she swept over to them. She greeted her as if she hadn't seen her in years.

Not sure why her friend was behaving so strangely, Jackie just went along with it. She also noticed that Caroline neglected to greet Logan and instead left that to Charles.

"You look wonderful!" Caroline held Jackie's arm akimbo to take in the dress. "Gucci? Very nice."

"Yes, it was a gift." Jackie smiled meaningfully at Logan.

Caroline's gaze flickered over to the man next to Jackie before her lips pursed in admiration. "Not bad."

"They outdid themselves in here." Jackie let her gaze wander once more.

"Gorgeous, isn't it? I'm very pleased." She pointed across the way at a table by the sand. "You're over there near us. Each couple gets their own table. Unless you dislike that arrangement." She added the last bit in a whisper.

Jackie nodded. "That's great."

"Then go ahead and take your seats or mingle if you like. We should eat once we make the speeches and all that."

Caroline never was one for speeches. She loved it when people took notice of her, but she didn't want to have to speak to get their attention. That was usually accomplished by her stunning looks. Nothing else was needed. Usually.

Charles nodded hello before his and Caroline's attentions were drawn elsewhere.

Logan returned to her side. "So what would you like to do?"

"Let's get some drinks."

"Sounds good." He put his hand at the small of her back and they walked to a table glittering with crystal glasses, some filled with drinks, others sparkling and void.

The bartender smiled as they approached. "What can I get you?"

Logan turned to her. "Ladies first."

"White wine, please. Half a glass."

Chuckling, Logan held up two fingers. "Make mine the same."

They picked up their drinks and headed toward their table, but kept walking beyond it into the sand. It wasn't like they were abandoning the party. There were several others out there as well. As far as nights in paradise went, it was perfect. The air was warm and fragrant, the sky dark, clear and full of stars.

Jackie held her drink out to Logan. "Can you hold this for a second?"

"Sure."

He took it as she slipped out of her shoes and stood, carrying them on one crooked finger.

"Thanks." She retrieved her glass. "I don't want to ruin the shoes."

He laughed. "If you do I'll buy you another pair. A dozen if you like. In every color of the rainbow."

"You certainly know how to appeal to a girl's heart." Jackie smiled and held her glass out to his.

"Cheers." He tapped his rim to hers before taking a sip.

Jackie did likewise.

"So I had a spa day planned for us tomorrow."

"After the wedding rehearsal, right?"

He gave her a wry smile. "Of course."

"Sounds great."

Logan noticed the enthusiasm wasn't quite there, but once she arrived Jackie would love it.

"Just come by my suite tomorrow morning."

"Does that mean I'm not invited to stay tonight?"

Logan grinned. "I didn't want to presume."

"I'll guess we'll just have to see how you play your cards tonight."

After what had happened when he showed up to escort her to dinner, he wasn't sure how the night would turn out. He thought he'd done pretty well with his choice of clothes and shoes. Only that had backfired quite badly. It had never occurred to him that she would take it that way.

Logan had picked out things that he remembered her liking. It never dawned to him that she would think that it was an attempt to change her in any way.

It was as though she was determined to take everything he said, every gesture he made, the wrong way. It was frustrating, but he never had been one to turn down a challenge.

Somehow it made winning her over even more of a prize. That was if he could eventually do it.

It seemed a bit more likely after her comment about the coming night.

Was Jackie going to try to be more open about herself?

He was making a leap with that one, but he could only hope.

He was going to drive himself crazy. Logan took a long breath. He would let Jackie decide the pace.

"You look serious."

"Do I?"

"I was just joking about tonight. If you'd rather have your space, that's fine."

Jackie's eyes were wide and he could clearly see the uncertainty. Was she testing the waters and seeking reassurance from him that it wasn't misplaced?

"Of course I want you to stay the night. There's nothing I want more."

Logan relieved her of her drink and placed it along with his in the sand, wiggling them deeper into it so they stayed upright. "Can I have this dance?"

"There's no one else dancing."

"So we'll be trendsetters." He held his arms out and waited for her to step into them.

When she put her shoes down and finally stepped into his embrace, Logan held her tightly to him and they swayed to the soft beat of the music.

The sensation of having her so close was blissful. Feeling her curves pressed against him tempted him to take things further, but he considered where they were and how important it was for Jackie to be there for Caroline. So he danced and did his best to ignore the burgeoning erection he knew she could feel against her.

"Hey, you two. We're sitting down for dinner."

Charles stayed a step away from the sand beckoning them to come in. The rest of the guests had already taken their seats. It seemed that they had missed the call to come in.

Jackie lurched from his arms. "Sorry, we'll be right there." She grabbed her shoes. "We should get in there."

Logan picked up their glasses and followed.

All eyes were on them as they took their seats. Jackie's cheeks were a bright pink and her eyes were averted as he helped her into her chair. A glance around the room proved they were the topic of conversation. He wished he could shield her from their speculative gazes.

As he thought about it, it occurred to him that she always seemed to be watched and whispered about among the people at the resort with them. It was strange that they paid such close attention to her. Even with all the new people in the room, she seemed to be favored with covert glances and nudges.

And Jackie knew it. She did her best not to appear as though she cared, but she did. Her shoulders were stiff and she doggedly kept her gaze away from everyone else's because she knew they watched her. Talked about her.

Logan stood where he was and glared at the room.

"What are you doing?" Jackie grabbed his arm and dragged him down into his seat.

"What the hell are they whispering about?" Was all the attention because of who she was spending time with?

"Just ignore them."

"But—" If it was because of him, he'd give them something to talk about.

"Logan, please. I just want to have a nice evening. I don't care what a few gossiping idiots have to say."

He gripped her hand when she tried to pull it away. "What are they saying? You must have some idea since this seems to happen to you all the time."

She stared at him mulishly. "I don't care. And neither should you."

"Jacqueline! You look wonderful!" Regina swept up to them and took Jackie's hands. "Gucci! Very nice!"

The tight smile Jackie gave the woman twisted Logan's gut.

"Thank you, Regina. It was a gift."

The woman chortled as if what she'd said was the most amusing thing Regina had ever heard. "Of course it was."

"I thought it was an occasion that called for the line's latest." Jackie eyed the woman's dress. "I guess that was my prerogative."

Logan smile smiled at the way Caroline's mother puffed up. She did well to recover, however. "It looks as though the speeches are about to start."

Charles' father stood at the center of the room and cleared his throat, drawing all eyes. Logan spared him a momentary glance before turning his attention back to Jackie. What wasn't she telling him?

Speeches were made and food was served. Logan didn't care about any of it.

Jackie kept quiet almost the entire time. She responded as she should, when she should, but it was mechanical, almost as if it was preprogrammed. Her smile was forced and she appeared to be all but completely checked out of the situation. Why was she forcing herself to be there?

For Caroline?

What did she owe her? As far as he'd ever seen, Jackie always seemed to be the one that did the helping.

Logan knew Jackie wouldn't answer anything while they were within earshot of everyone. He would have to bide his time. Maybe she would be open to discussion later.

If she wasn't completely stressed out by the meal, that was.

It was certainly stressing him out enough. Logan could only imagine what Jackie was going through.

No wonder she was always so wound up. And then he would show up and push her buttons more.

Was it any wonder why she would fly off the handle? She was completely frazzled just being there.

He was just the icing on the cake.

Logan would make sure that the next two days would be more relaxing for her. Tomorrow especially.

Jackie focused on the food, the table, a spot in the distance behind whoever's turn it was to speak.

Next to her, Logan sat jaw tense, fists clenched. She was sure if anyone was to venture close enough to their table they would probably get dragged over and interrogated.

Unsure of whether his protectiveness was welcome or not, Jackie just prayed that people would take the hint and stop staring.

He was sure to ask questions after this. The time they'd spent together so far had almost been exclusively alone. But now that he'd seen how others reacted when they were around her, how could he not want to know what was going on? She knew she would.

Why couldn't everyone just mind their own business and stop being so interested in what others were doing for just once?

Tough luck with this crowd. Most of the people at the meal tonight were ones who had flown in for the ceremony. So of course they had to catch up on what was going on. Who was there.

With the fallen Jaqueline Pennington in the room, what else was there to talk about?

At least her parents hadn't been invited. That would have been insufferable. Though seeing her with Logan would have outraged them in a way she would have loved to have seen.

Logan nudged her. "What are you smirking about?"

"I'll tell you another time."

"I wish you'd tell me now. It'd make this fish a lot easier to swallow."

Jackie rolled her eyes. "If you didn't want the fish, why didn't you just tell someone?" She swapped dishes with him, exchanging her steak with his fish.

"The other guy ordered the fish, not me. I'm just here as a stand-in, remember?" He sawed off a bit of the steak and ate it with an appreciative groan. "So good."

She smiled. "You should have said something sooner. You have more to eat now." Jackie had been so preoccupied that she hadn't checked to see how he was doing. Not that it was her place. He was a grown man.

Then again, he had been out of sorts himself. With everything going on it was a miracle they'd even managed to eat at all.

"I'll be fine. It's not like this place doesn't have outstanding room service."

That was true enough. She would miss it once it was over and she was back in her real life.

"And now you're sad again."

Her gaze collided with his. "Stop scrutinizing me and enjoy your meal."

When he said nothing, she turned to find him still watching her. "What did I just say?"

"How can I stop watching you? You're the most beautiful woman in the room and the biggest mystery."

"Is that what you want? A big mystery to unravel?" Of course that was why he was being so attentive.

"Not at all. I was just thinking that I'm the luckiest guy in the room to have the complete package right here next to me."

"Will you just stop?" Heat crept into her cheeks once again. How was it that after everything they'd done, he could still make her blush with a few words?

"It's the truth." He washed down the last of the steak with what was left of his wine. "Think we've put in enough time here yet?"

"Not even remotely." There was going to be mingling and more dreaded conversation to come.

"If people want to talk to you rather than about you, they'll have time tomorrow at the rehearsal or at the reception after the big event." He stood and held up his hand. "Come on."

Jackie slipped her hand into his with a smile. But instead of letting him lead her from the room immediately she dragged him over to Caroline and Charles.

The instant her friend saw her approach, her expression became pinched. "Are you okay?"

Jackie nodded. "We're going to take off. But we'll see you in the morning for the rehearsal."

Caroline came around the table to give her a hug. "No one's hounding you, are they?" she whispered.

"No, just getting the usual stares and all that. Nothing I can't handle."

"Busybodies with no lives of their own," she snarled. Caroline drew back and looked at Logan then back at Jackie. "We'll see you both in the morning."

Logan mumbled something but she didn't catch it. They wound their way through the crowded room and it wasn't until they made it out that Jackie felt like she could breathe again. She let the rigid smile fall from her face as she sighed with relief.

"You know I'm completely confused by what's going on, right? That I want to ask you about it?"

"I'd be disappointed if you didn't." She tried to keep her voice light but she failed if his expression was anything to go by.

"I won't yet. I hope you'll tell me on your own, when you feel ready. You hardly need someone getting in your face right now." Logan closed his hand around hers and held it tightly to his chest. "Just know that if you need someone to back you up, I'm the guy."

The smile that spread over her lips was a true one. "I know. Thanks."

He pressed her hand to his lips. "Good. So where do you want to go now? It's still early. We could wander around for a bit."

"Any other secret little places around here you haven't shown me yet?"

He smiled mysteriously. "How about we just start walking and see where our feet take us?"

"These aren't exactly walking shoes, though." Jackie kicked back one foot to lift in demonstration.

"Take them off."

Jackie pouted. "I'm not about to go walking around here without my shoes on."

"That's not what I said to do, was it? Will you just take them off?"

Huffing and using him for support, she slipped the shoes off. "Now what?"

"Give them to me."

She did.

Logan hunkered down in front of her. "Now get on my back."

"You're joking."

Craning his head around to smile at her he asked, "Does it look like I'm joking?"

What the hell? Might as well give people something new to talk about. Jackie climbed on. Once Logan had her held securely against him he stood and started walking outside.

"So are you at least going to tell me where we're off to?"

"It wouldn't be much of a secret if I told you, would it?"

The air here was something Jackie would never tire of. She felt the same way about being wrapped around Logan. Despite their ups and downs this week, he had proven himself loyal, gentle and even understanding on top of being her dream lover. It was wonderful and scary. It would be so easy to just let go and fall back into his arms.

And why shouldn't she?

The one thing holding her back was their past. The hurt he'd inflicted upon her had been terrible. But hadn't it led her to a life she now enjoyed? She had become independent and, while she was inhibited by her lack of cash a lot of the time, she was free to be and do what she wanted, like she'd always dreamed. The one thing that was missing was Logan by her side.

Now, if he was willing, they could be a couple.

But she had to find out why he had left her in the first place. Why he had disappeared as he did. Until she found out the truth behind that, Jackie couldn't trust him completely.

At least not with her heart.

He walked onto the sand. Jackie couldn't sense anyone else on the beach with them. She suspected that most of the people staying at the resort were there for Caroline's wedding and were at the dinner. The inky darkness beckoned them to venture farther. Jackie simply held on for the ride. She lowered her head to rest her chin in the crook of his neck and closed her eyes.

His scent was intoxicating. Combined with the darkness and the rhythmic surge of the surf it was downright hypnotic.

They walked a little while longer, before he jostled her.

"Are you asleep?"

Jackie sighed. "Nope. Just enjoying the ride."

Chuckling, he adjusted his grip on her legs. "I'm going to put you down now, okay?"

"Yup."

Logan slowly slid her down his back so she stood in the soft sand.

She curled her toes into the powdery sand and burrowed her feet deeper into the warmth. They stood in a little alcove that hid them from the hotel. The ocean spread before them like ink under a velvet sky glittering with stars. There was no moon, yet it wasn't too dark to see.

Jackie didn't get much of a chance to relish the feeling before he spun her in his arms, cupped her cheeks and kissed the breath from her lungs.

He smiled against her lips before he withdrew. "I've been wanting to do that all night."

"Well, in that case." She dragged him back in for another. Jackie took the lead, brushing her tongue against his as she pressed herself against him.

Logan didn't miss a beat and angled his head to deepen the kiss. He pulled her tight against him, allowing no space between them. As if he wanted to fuse them together.

The kiss was nearly hot enough to do it.

He picked her up. Jackie wound her legs around his hips as he walked back toward the stone that hid them from sight.

He muttered against her lips as he shrugged off his jacket. "Hang on tight with your legs."

Logan slipped it off and whipped it around behind her. She jammed her arms into the sleeves just as he pressed her against the rock. He pushed her skirt up and out of the way so he could run his hands over her thighs and grip her ass.

Holding her in place, he ground his rigid cock against her. The searing heat emanating from him penetrated their clothes.

Jackie rocked her pelvis, creating a friction that wasn't nearly enough. But it was something at least. Logan joined in, rubbing himself against her in counterpoint to her movements. Much better, but Jackie needed more.

Tugging at his belt, she quickly undid it and the fastening on his trousers. With them out of her way she guided her hand under to curl around his cock. She pumped her hand up and down his length, tightening her grip as he grew harder.

"Shit, Jackie. Keep that up and I'll come way too soon."

She didn't slow, loving the power she had over him. Grinning, Jackie sucked his bottom lip between hers, giving it a little bite.

Growling, Logan wrenched aside her panties and circled her clit. He was rougher in his touch than usual but she loved it. She would come before he would if he kept it up. And he knew it.

Sparks entered the periphery of her vision. Her breath hitched as she got closer to a quick orgasm. Just as she began to tremble, Logan withdrew his hand. Somehow he managed to find and don a condom before pushing his entire length into her with one hard thrust.

Jackie came spectacularly on his second thrust, groaning as she shattered around him.

Logan held her tight, keeping her from falling bonelessly to the ground as he sought his own release. Mindlessly, he pounded into her. Each impact against her clit sent more shock waves radiating through Jackie which culminated in another climax just as Logan orgasmed as well.

She clung to him as the pleasure subsided.

Trembling like she was, Logan pulled her away from the rock. "Are you okay?"

Her hips and butt were a bit tender, but other than that, she felt wonderful as she always did after sex with Logan. "I'm good."

He lowered her to her feet so they could right their clothes before he tugged her into his embrace. "Feel like sitting here a while?"

Considering how loose she felt, that sounded ideal. "I would love it."

Logan put himself between her and the rock and positioned Jackie between his thighs with her back to his chest.

In her warm cocoon, Jackie felt safe and so comfortable. Definitely a sensations she wanted more of. Logan wrapped his arms around her shoulders with a happy-sounding sigh.

"This is nice, isn't it?" His voice rumbled through her.

"It is." Jackie let her head tip to rest against his shoulder.

"So have I convinced you to come to my suite with me?"

She slumped to the side a bit to look up at him. "So that was your ploy, was it?"

"You caught me." He chuckled.

It was so simple. They complemented each other so well. Logan felt right. She felt right when she was with him.

They sat quietly for a long while. For Jackie, it was incredibly soothing to listen to the waves and Logan's steady heartbeat.

He lowered his nose to her hair and inhaled deeply. "You smell wonderful."

Jackie giggled. "You don't smell so bad yourself."

He froze.

"What?"

"I think I hear someone coming our way."

Logan quickly got to his feet and helped Jackie do the same. They were up and with the clothes righted just as another couple rounded the rock.

"Oh!" The woman almost tripped over her man in her surprise. "Sorry."

"It's all yours." Logan took Jackie's hand and led her away. When they were out of earshot he leaned closer. "Was that the same couple from the beach?"

Jackie pressed her hand to her mouth to quieten the laugh. "I have no idea. Could be."

"I guess he's trying to make it up to her."

She snickered. "If he was trying to make it up to her he might have rethought the sand."

"I never hear you complain."

"Because you don't give me anything to complain about while we're on the sand. That guy, on the other hand…"

His laughter joined hers. "Well, I'm glad to hear you have no complaints. I'm quite proud, actually."

She looked at the way his chest had puffed up. "You don't say."

"So I take pride in my ability to please you. So sue me."

She just hoped she made him feel the same way.

When they reached the point where sand met stone, they paused so she could put her shoes back on, then they slowly wandered along the paths back up to his suite.

Finally, Jackie felt as though she was on vacation.

Like she was more than just a shadow of a person.

Chapter Ten

Logan woke with his limbs tangled with Jackie's. He felt something that he could only call contentedness suffusing his entire being. Would every morning be like this waking up next to Jackie?

Not that the night was worse. They'd made love long into the early hours and it had been sublime. Jackie had been with him every step of the way. Her response to him was nothing short of incredible. She made him feel like a god.

A feeling he wouldn't mind experiencing again.

Logan nuzzled her neck and smiled when her breathing changed rhythm and she arched into his body.

"Good morning." He grazed the delicate skin of her throat with his teeth. "Sleep well?"

She sighed. "Very." Jackie rolled over to give him a sleepy smile. "But that shouldn't be surprising considering the workout I had the night before."

Logan gave her a lingering kiss, which she returned wholeheartedly, winding herself around him.

She chuckled when her hand grazed his burgeoning erection. "Feels like you're about ready for another round."

"Only if you're interested."

Jackie kissed him slowly teasing him with her tongue. "I think I can be persuaded."

"That's what I like to hear."

He cupped her breasts and slid down to kiss one then the other. "You are gorgeous."

Jackie laughed. "Right."

"You are!" He sucked a nipple between his lips and flicked her with his tongue before he said, "And absolutely delicious."

The way she was smiling was contagious, but he could see she wasn't fully convinced. If she didn't believe him, he'd just have to prove to her that he found her irresistible.

Logan lavished attention on her breasts for a while longer. Not that it was any hardship. He kissed a path down from the valley between her breasts to her belly button. Then farther down.

Jackie readily parted her thighs for him allowing him access to do whatever he liked. His chest felt full that she was giving herself to him so freely now.

He took a moment to look at her glistening folds. So pretty. Logan pressed his lips to her, using his tongue to gently find her clit.

"Logan…"

Jackie's thighs quaked as he sucked her clit rhythmically.

Her escalating cries were music to his ears until she reached her peak and screamed her release.

His cock throbbed when he slid back up her body. Logan couldn't get enough of her. He found it wasn't just his body that constantly craved more of Jackie. He wanted her there when she wasn't around.

He fished a condom out of the bedside table and rolled it on. Jackie surprised him by shoving him over and straddling his hips. Her mischievous smile had him wondering what she planned.

Jackie gazed down at Logan, admiring his handsome face and superb body. And he was at her mercy.

The possibilities running through her mind were delicious, but she was most interested in another orgasm and this time making it mutual.

She angled him just so and slid him back and forth over her slit, lubricating the broad head of his cock with her juices. Logan lay beneath her, surprisingly docile. He was usually the aggressor, and she wasn't sure just how he would take her assuming the more dominant role.

From the way he was smiling, Logan seemed to like it.

Jackie slowly slid herself down his erection, impaling herself upon him. The sensation of his stretching her, filling her so completely, was a wonder in itself. When he was a deep as he could go, she angled her hips to take him just a little farther.

She paused a moment to savor how he felt embedded so far inside her.

Logan groaned, rocking his hips slightly forcing her to move to keep balance, which earned her another moan from him. "You're killing me, Jackie."

He wasn't the only one. She needed this as much as he did.

She rose up on her knees a little and dropped down onto him. Jackie did it experimentally a few times, before Logan gripped her hips and pulled her down over him—hard. It sent shock waves through her, and her breath caught in her lungs.

Logan guided her movements, helping her find a rhythm and showing her how to please them both.

He watched her with heavy lidded eyes, his lips parting as his own breathing quickened. "I hope you're almost there, because I'm getting close."

As if he had to ask. Jackie closed her eyes as she let her head fall back. She orgasmed with a keening cry as he surged into her and reached his own peak with a shout.

She dropped forward to rest against his chest. His rapid heartbeat and breath mirrored her own.

Logan wrapped his arms around her. "That's certainly one way to wake up."

She laughed and tried to slide off him, but he wouldn't let her budge.

"Just a minute longer," he grumbled.

Jackie relented, enjoying the connection as much as he obviously did.

"What time is it?"

"Don't know. Don't care."

She could barely make herself care too, but they did have a schedule to keep to, at least until after the rehearsal. Then they were free to do whatever they liked. Which reminded her about his mysterious plans for today.

"What have you got planned for us today?"

He cracked open one eye. "You'll have to wait and see."

"You're infuriating, you know that?"

"I know of a way to change that opinion if you're willing to give me a few minutes to recuperate."

"Funny." He was, though, and she was smiling when she slid off him to nestle against his side.

They had left the doors open, and she could clearly see the sky had just begun to brighten. They had more than enough time to laze around for a while.

"I'm just going to tidy myself up." Logan slid out of bed and walked to the bathroom. He stuck his head out. "You can always join me for a shower."

She wondered what his shower would be like. The one in her room was fantastic. His could only be mind-blowing.

"I'll be right there." She gave him a few minutes before she walked in.

As she suspected, the room was much larger than hers. The rough stone and large windows gave the room the feel of being in nature while at the same time still protecting the modesty of anyone within.

The shower was situated above the huge sunken tub and Logan had already turned the water to cascade hard and fast from the massive shower head directly above.

"Well, your bathroom definitely trumps mine."

He laughed as he took her hand and helped her into the tub. Made of stone as it was, the tub had been polished smooth and felt warm and satiny to the touch.

He stood at the side watching the water run down her body for a moment before there was a knock at the door.

"It's a bit early for someone to be knocking, isn't it?"

The smile on his face piqued her curiosity but he held up his hand. "Stay there. I'll be right back." He made sure she wasn't about to move before wrapping a towel around himself and going to answer.

What did he have up his sleeve this time?

Jackie wanted to give into her curiosity, but held off. Whatever he had planned was important enough for him to plan it this early. She'd let him have it. She reached for the hotel's signature toiletries. The large frosted aqua-blue bottles were capped with silver seashells. She found the body wash, shampoo and conditioner, and dragged them all closer, along with the softest washcloths she'd ever touched.

By the time she had washed and conditioned her hair, Logan had reappeared.

He dropped his towel, and she nearly dropped the bottle she had just picked up.

With a grin he stepped in next to her. "Let me help."

She let her eyes drift close as he slathered the body wash over her skin. He traced patterns on her skin with his big, warm hands, slowing to spend much of his time on her breasts, her ass, between her thighs.

Jackie captured globs of foam and glided her hands over him, wanting to tease and torture him as much as she was her.

"So, have you got what you wanted sorted in the other room?" She grazed her hand over his ass.

"Nice try." Logan cupped her breasts, squeezing them gently.

"I was just asking a question." She blinked up at him innocently as she soaped his thighs.

He flicked his thumbs over her nipples, coaxing them into hard points. "Uh huh. Right."

Jackie circled his groin, staying well away from his rigid erection. Instead, she raked her nails over his rippling abs and up to graze his pecs. She followed up with her tongue, licking the water from his skin before lightly biting his nipple.

"You can torture me all you like, you're getting nothing." He grinned at her—clearly her method of 'torture' was pleasurable to him.

She would see how long he'd last if she pushed him a little further. Jackie slid down his body, letting her hands bump over his muscles as she went. Holding his gaze, she licked her lips and grasped his erection in her hand, cupping his balls with her other.

"Torture me all you want. I'm not telling you a thing," he rasped.

A chuckle bubbled up her throat as she flicked her tongue over the tip of his erection and a shudder rippled through him. When she closed her mouth over the broad head of his cock and sucked, he wobbled a little. She smiled at him again before she began sucking and bobbing her head in earnest.

Logan groaned and gripped her hair to quicken her pace when she added her hands to the mix. She pushed him to the edge of his control as quickly as he was able to do to her.

It didn't take long before she felt his balls draw up in her hand and his cock grow bigger, harder, in her mouth. Logan dragged her forward, driving himself deeply as he came on a shuddering moan of her name.

Jackie swallowed his release as quickly as she could, but felt some escape and slide down her chin. When his orgasm finally wound down he slipped himself from her mouth and smiled at her, biting his bottom lip as he wiped his thumb over hers. He dragged his cum back to her mouth and she licked it off with long strokes of her tongue.

"God, Jackie. You have no idea what you do to me."

Logan dragged her up so he could wind his arms around her. Pressed tightly against him, Jackie listened to the thudding of his heart.

He angled them under the shower, fully rinsing off what remained of the suds.

Logan picked her up and stepped up out of the shower to gather her up in a thick, luxurious towel that might as well have been a blanket. Wrapping it around herself, she tucked it securely between her breasts and watched as he clung his around his lean hips.

It was when he turned off the shower that she heard the music coming from the other room.

Jackie gave him a questioning glance as she opened the door to get a peek.

Housekeeping had obviously been there. The room had been tidied, the bed made, and the flowers swapped out for another vivid array. What surprised her was set up in the bedroom was a massage table and a little table laden with bottles of oil. Incense burned from sticks dotted around the room and music that matched what had played at the spa came from speakers hidden from her view.

"So what do you think?"

How could she not like it? "It's wonderful."

"I figured we could get one of my fantasies out of my system."

"Naked all day?"

"As much of the day as we can manage." He wiggled his eyebrows. "We can get some breakfast. Head to the rehearsal then hurry back here."

Laughing, she walked into his waiting arms. "Sounds perfect." And it would get her fantasy of him massaging her properly to become a reality as well.

"Did you want room service or should we head down to the restaurant?"

"Maybe we should stretch our legs for a bit?" Jackie didn't foresee them being on their feet much for the rest of the day. At least they wouldn't if she had her way.

Jackie couldn't keep the smile from curving her lips. Even when she realized that the only thing she had to wear was the dress from the night before, it couldn't be wiped from her face.

She slipped into the dress and turned so he could help zip her up. Which he did without fail. But instead of letting her go, he pulled her in for a bear hug. Jackie laughed as she tried to wriggle out of his grasp. "I've got to go back to my suite for a change of clothes."

"I suppose wearing something of mine would be out of the question."

Jackie could only imagine what kind of response that would cause. It would be just as bad, if not worse, than if she wore the same dress again.

"I'll meet you downstairs."

Logan rasped his stubble against her neck. "Hurry."

Giving him a quick kiss and making sure to draw back before things got out of hand, she rushed to her room. The thought of Logan being so impatient to be with her again made her smile. Being wanted by someone she wanted just as much felt wonderful.

She dashed through the halls and pathways. Trying to keep her gait quick but as dignified as possible was hard, considering she just wanted to sprint as fast as she could to get to her room, get changed and meet up with him again.

On the way, she got a text from Caroline saying that she needed to speak with her urgently. Jackie knew she should reply, but her friend would just have to wait. At least until she got changed. With one day to go, Caroline was probably in a panicked state.

Images of what she would be like in Caroline's place if she was getting ready to marry Logan flitted into her mind. Would she be as freaked out as her friend? She wanted to believe that she would be as happy, calm and content as she was in that moment.

But she was jumping way ahead.

She rushed into her suite and dug through her suitcase for something casual yet cute. The best she could come up with was a pair of dark, wide-legged trousers that could do with an ironing and a floaty pink top. They would have to do for today. It wasn't like she was walking a runway at a fashion show.

She changed, carefully putting the dress Logan bought her back into the garment bag and delicately replacing the shoes in their box.

Jackie pulled her hair back into a ponytail and applied makeup lightly, enough to accentuate.

It took a second to give herself one last look before she grabbed her purse and strode out. She texted Caroline with the usual affirmations and a promise to meet up later. More specifically, that evening.

She shoved her phone into her purse just as she reached the restaurant. It occurred to her that she hadn't specified which restaurant, and yet Logan had come to the right one and got them a table near the aquarium.

He stood as she approached. He had shaved and was now dressed in a white button-down and a pair of jeans. Logan looked great. So handsome.

He gave her a peck on the cheek before guiding her to the seat next to his. "I ordered for you. I hope you don't mind."

"Not at all." She settled in and took a sip of the ice water waiting for her. Toying with the lemon slice on the surface, she looked at him. "So what did you order?"

"Crepes and coffee. Is that good for you?"

"Wonderful."

He took her hand and tangled his fingers with hers. That was it. Just seeking contact with her. It was as though it was something they did every day. It was comfortable.

It was perfect.

Logan was her man. It was something she thought she knew years ago, but now she was positive. Logan Forrester was the man she was meant to be with.

The revelation was as awe-inspiring as it was stunning.

What if he didn't feel the same way?

Her chest ached at the thought.

He had to after their time tougher the past few days, how could he not? Then again, men didn't exactly think the same way. For him it'd probably just been good sex.

She took another long sip of her water, nearly choking on the lemon when she convulsively swallowed.

Logan immediately patted her gently on the back. "You okay?"

"Fine," she gasped. She heaved a breath and forced herself to smile.

Logan didn't look convinced. "Are you sure? Because you're really pale."

Jackie nodded, even though she wasn't entirely sure herself. Was she going to be all right? How was she even going to talk to him about it? Especially with everything still hanging over them. It was entirely possible that he would want to stick to their agreed arrangement and want things to end when this trip did.

But he was being so sweet.

Hadn't she thought the same of him when he'd broken her heart?

It was pointless speculating. She was going to drive herself crazy if she kept it up.

As she tried to figure out a way of broaching the subject with him, the crepes arrived. They'd buy her a little more time.

Logan watched Jackie as she cut the crepes into ribbons, barely eating any. Something was up. She had seemed happy when she arrived then in a flash, she had gone quiet and pensive.

After the night they'd had, Logan was sure she felt as fantastic as he did. The wall that had been between them was crumbling, and she seemed to truly relax with him.

So what had just happened?

He could almost see her mind at work, and there had definitely been a thought that had caused her to shut him out.

Logan stabbed his crepe before cutting off a hunk with his fork. "Is your breakfast to your liking?"

"It's very nice." Jackie kept her gaze on her food as she spoke.

"If there's something on your mind, I'd love to hear it." He put his fork down and sat back in his chair.

Jackie stilled for an instant. She swallowed the mouthful of crepe then washed it down with a gulp of water before she sat back as well.

It was the longest ten seconds of his life.

"Where do you see this going, Logan?"

Her voice was choked, barely a whisper.

He saw it going all the way. Logan wasn't about to propose marriage right then and there, but he could see it going that far once again.

The last thing he wanted to do was freak her out by going too fast. It was better to go slowly. "Why do you ask?"

"I just wondered. I feel as though things have gone beyond our original agreement when we first started this."

He allowed himself a smile. "I think so, too."

Jackie smiled a little as well, and the tightness in his chest eased a bit.

The mood shifted yet again. Though, Logan wasn't sure how he wanted to segue into how they were going to proceed. There was still a lot they needed to sort out between them. But if he was willing to get over what had happened, he couldn't see why she would have a problem.

From now on, he envisioned smooth sailing. At least that was the hope. Being with Jackie again was nothing short of miraculous. He wasn't going to do anything to screw it up.

Jackie relaxed visibly and the mood slowly altered once again. They reverted to two lovers enjoying the morning together.

They leisurely enjoyed their meal, adding another cup of coffee each at the end. Not many words were spoken. Logan didn't feel like they were needed. Every touch and look said volumes.

Jackie checked her phone for the time and gasped. "We're going to be late!"

How had they whiled away so much time? And yet it felt as though no time had passed at all.

He stood and held his hand out to her. "I guess we'd better get a move on."

She grabbed her things and took his hand with her free one. Logan was sure their lack of time management would stress her out, but she didn't look too concerned. In fact, she looked calmer than he thought she would. Up until now, she had been a stickler for time keeping, especially where the wedding was concerned. This morning she seemed concerned but not completely obsessed with getting there.

Or perhaps she wasn't overly concerned with getting away from him.

He couldn't help the smile from creeping over his lips.

They arrived at the beach where everyone was waiting.

Almost everyone.

Jackie looked up and down obviously searching for her friend. But Caroline and Charles were nowhere to be seen.

Caroline's mother rushed over. "Jacqueline, have you seen or heard from Caroline?"

Guilt crept over Jackie's face. "I had a text, but nothing since then." She pulled out her phone and checked again.

"She and Charles are probably holed up somewhere and lost track of time." Logan offered.

A man who Logan assumed would be officiating the ceremony walked up to them. "I have to be across the island within the next hour. If we are to do this practice run we need to do it now."

"How can we do it without the bride and groom?" Caroline's mother stared wide-eyed at the man.

The harassed-looking coordinator appeared at that moment and forced a bright smile. "We can have this couple stand in for them. I'm assuming they are part of the wedding party."

Jackie nodded, but all color had drained from her face. "Would that be appropriate? They're the ones who need to know what to do."

"Please, Jacqueline. It won't take up too much time and then you two could relay the information to Caroline and Charles. Though they already know what to do anyway. It's their ceremony. They're the ones who planned it out."

Logan just nodded. "Sure. We'll do it."

He dragged Jackie with him to the podium that was acting as the altar. "What's going on with Caroline and Charles?" he whispered.

"I have no idea. I got a text this morning saying she needed to talk to me, but I haven't heard from her since. You don't think they've taken off, do you?"

"I'm sure they wouldn't leave their families in the lurch like that." He might have said the words, but he didn't feel too confident in them.

"I should have gone to find her the moment I got the text." Jackie looked anguished and it broke his heart a little.

"It'll work out. We'll just stand in for them now and if we haven't heard from them by the end of it, we'll search for them."

"Okay." She didn't look convinced.

"If you two will take your places." The coordinator motioned them over, positioning them very precisely. She linked their hands. "Pretend to be in love." Then she rushed off to get everyone else in their places.

The woman might have said it jokingly, but when Jackie's gaze collided with Logan's, everything else fell away.

Jackie barely listened to what was being said or going on around them. They went through the motions of the ceremony. And while she was concerned about her friend, she couldn't help but wonder at the surreal turn things had taken.

She stood holding Logan's hands, pretending to be getting married like a bizarre parody of a children's game.

The officiant said whatever it was he was supposed to say. Jackie heard words like 'love' and 'eternal'. All she saw was Logan and the look in his eyes as they were being said. His warm hands closed around hers made her feel safe.

Made it feel authentic.

"And here's where they would say 'I do'."

Jackie murmured the words before she knew what she was doing. What was even more startling was Logan had said them too.

The feeling that left her with was hard to identify but left her heart fluttering in her chest.

Logan cleared his throat with a cough.

The wedding coordinator grinned brightly and walked them through the final steps of the ceremony, while Jackie robotically went through the motions.

"And there you go! Just like that, Charles and Caroline will be Mr. and Mrs. Sutcliffe!"

Not that anyone was listening to her any longer. Jackie looked up at Logan and realized she still held onto his hand. When she tried to pull it back, he wouldn't let her.

That moment had shaken him too, apparently. There was something in his eyes that caused her insides to tremble. The ceremony, as fake as it was, felt right. Real.

He took a long slow breath and brought her hand to his lips.

He brushed his lips lightly over the back of her fingers. "I guess we should try and find the wayward couple, shouldn't we?"

Jackie nodded. "Let me check my phone."

He held her hand a moment longer before relinquishing it.

She quickly dug through her purse for her phone, but before she fished it out Caroline's mother let out a delighted squeal. "They're fine. They went on an early morning excursion and their boat lost power. It's being fixed and they should be back in a couple of hours."

Jackie sagged with relief. "Thank goodness."

Logan smiled a little as well. "Shall we, then?"

They would head back to his suite now that Caroline and Charles were okay. Maybe they would talk a little about what had just happened?

She slipped her hand into his. The frisson of electricity that zapped between them told her talking was probably going to be pushed aside in favor of more sensual activities.

They made it to his suite quickly. No words were exchanged or needed. Logan closed the door securely behind them and started unbuttoning his shirt. Not wanting to be left behind, Jackie slipped her top off over her head.

It quickly turned into a game of who could get undressed the quickest and within moments they stood bare.

She let her gaze wander over him. His body was perfectly proportioned, well sculpted and beautiful. Jackie could spend all day just staring at him. Well, not quite all day, because just looking at him stirred other longings. Ones that involved touching and tasting what she saw.

Jackie stepped into his arm and angled her head to receive a sizzling kiss. She let her hands glide over his chest, exploring the taut skin over his pecs. The groan that rumbled through him when she grazed his flat nipples with her thumbs brought a smile to her lips.

She had just as much power over him as he had over her and it was a heady thing. That she could have a big, virile man like Logan trembling and groaning from something as simple as a touch of her fingers was amazing — awe-inspiring, even.

Logan cupped her cheek and brushed his lips against hers again. When he drew back and gazed into her eyes, Jackie's breath caught.

The look there, it was one she remembered glowing back at her before. Trembling, she stared right back into his eyes, not quite daring to believe what she saw.

Love.

As simple as that. It was right there in his eyes, shining brightly.

Too choked up for words, Jackie grinned up at him and dragged him in for another kiss, hoping he knew she returned his feelings.

Logan kissed her long, lingeringly before he picked her up and carried her to the massage table.

The last thing on her mind was a massage. When he placed her down on it she hooked her legs around his, keeping him from going anywhere. After grabbing a bottle of oil, she pulled out the stopper and drizzled it over her breasts, watching him the entire time.

Logan licked his lips as he used both hands to rub the oil into her skin. He slowly spread the warmed liquid from her collarbone to her pelvis. He smoothed it in thoroughly, obviously loving the feel of her skin against his as much as she did.

Slowly, he slid down her body until he knelt between her legs. He greased up her legs, starting at her toes. Rubbing them one by one then sliding up to her ankles, her calves then thighs. Reverently making sure every inch of her was oiled and pliant.

Jackie allowed him to do what he liked. She was too boneless to do anything but. Having Logan's hands all over her, caressing her everywhere, was everything she had imagined and more.

The liquid ache at her core was growing by the second. Logan seemed to read her mind because he lowered his head to kiss her between the thighs. Without drawing back, he opened his mouth to suck her clit between his lips and flick her gently with his tongue.

It was all she need to come shuddering to a climax. Jackie gripped his head as she reared against Logan's mouth. Starbursts exploded in her vision as he continued his sensual assault. Her orgasm continued on and on until her vision dimmed and she had to pull him away from her over-sensitized flesh.

Logan dragged her off the table to sprawl over him on the floor. The oil allowed her to glide over him pleasurably. He reached into the clothing he'd discarded and fished out a condom and put it on before he angled her and slid her over him.

Jackie gasped as he filled her in one swift thrust. Taking advantage of the oil, he slid her back and forth over him. The strange sensation caused by the slippery friction was indescribably good. Logan began to meet her with a thrust whenever he slid her down, each time sending radiating sparks of pleasure through her entire body.

It didn't take long for her to build to another orgasm. Jackie wanted him to come with her. Holding his gaze, she took control of the thrusts, the timing, the depth, the force. Logan watched her with utter fascination and delight on his face.

As her own orgasm started to tingle in her toes, his breath began to hitch. His hands clutched her hips as his jaw went slack. Gripping her to him, he sat up so that they were nearly face to face as their orgasms hit almost simultaneously.

The world blurred as Jackie trembled. Logan tangled his fingers in her hair, angling her head for a delicious kiss.

"You are incredible."

Jackie laughed, enjoying the closeness she felt with him. "I could say the same about you."

"I'm glad you think so." He refused to let go when she wriggled. "Just let me hold you a little bit longer."

She relented. It was a wonderful feeling. They stayed that way for a long while, just entwined with each other.

He carefully got to his feet, taking her with him as if she weighed nothing.

"Where are we going?" She giggled.

"To the shower." He shifted his grip as he started walking. "We're going to get clean before we get dirty again."

Chapter Eleven

Jackie woke the next morning entangled with Logan again, though this time he was sprawled over her. Smiling, she stretched slightly, loving the feel of his skin against hers, but not wanting to wake him. He mumbled something and wrapped his arms tighter around her, refusing to let her go even in sleep.

That he was so tired wasn't a surprise. They had had a long and very busy night. She couldn't muster the strength to do more than sigh.

The breeze that blew in was warm and fragrant, mingling with the lingering scent of the incense from the night before. The scenery outside shone brightly.

What time was it?

Jackie tried to reach her phone, but couldn't thanks to the weight of Logan pinning her down.

"Logan."

"Hmm?" He arched against her, giving her no doubt that his body was awake and ready to go, even if he wasn't.

"I think we slept in." Feeling him hot and hard against her severely tested her resolve to get out of bed.

"I think we can stand to stay in bed a little longer."

Sleep-rumpled, Logan looked adorable.

When she scowled at him he shrugged, completely unfazed. "It can't be that late. And the wedding isn't until this afternoon anyway."

It would be so easy to let him talk her into staying. "And you think that all I have to do is throw on a dress and that's all there is to it?"

"Well, yeah. You look amazing with makeup and without. In a dress" — he whipped aside the sheets to look at her — "and out of one."

"You're insatiable."

"Only for you." He wedged himself between her thighs and used his superior size to keep her in place. "Check the time. I promise we're not going to be late for anything."

As she reached for her phone, he grazed her breasts with his hands before cupping them firmly and nuzzling his nose between them.

And how was she going to read the damn thing if she couldn't see straight?

It took her a few tries to focus her eyes and keep them from rolling back from the pleasure coursing through her from his touch.

"So?" His voice was muffled against her skin.

He was right. They still had an hour at least before they had to get up. "We have a little time."

He lifted his gaze to catch hers with a small smirk. "Is that a challenge?"

Jackie wriggled under him. "Think you have what it takes to make me come before we have to leave?"

"Oh, I know I do." He lazily traced circles around her clit, sending tremors though her, proving his point. "The question is, can you get me to come to fit in with your time frame?"

That was interesting. Jackie had to admit she was intrigued. She knew she had an effect on him. But could she make him climax as quickly as he could make her?

Jackie ran her hands over him. "And if I do?"

"Then I shall hail you as queen of my world."

She reached his groin and closed her hand around his erection. "Does that mean you don't already?"

He groaned. "I will do it in front of the world."

She would love to see that happen. "You're on."

Jackie shoved him back to twist Logan under her.

He grinned up at her. "I like this whole dominatrix thing you've got going on right now."

She hushed him. "Shhh. I'm on a deadline."

"Yes, ma'am." He settled back ready to let her do whatever she wanted.

Jackie grabbed a condom from the bedside table and slid down his body to come face to face with his cock. Proud and erect, it was more than ready for her. Jackie gave the tip a sucking kiss before rolling the condom down over him.

Swinging her leg over his hips, she mounted him, sliding him deep into her.

Slowly, she began to rock up and down. She watched with satisfaction when his jaw hung slack as the sensations washed over him. Jackie knew exactly what he was feeling because the same thing was coursing through her.

Reaching behind her, Jackie cupped his balls, rolling them gently in her hand as she rode him, knowing he loved it when she did it.

"You're playing dirty."

"I'm winning." She chuckled, but gasped when he jerked upward suddenly, sending a spike of pleasure straight through her.

Obviously he wasn't about to give in so easily.

He closed his hands around her hips as he ground himself against her, inside her. He matched her rocking with thrusts that precisely hit a spot deep inside that caused her thighs to tremble.

Jackie wasn't going to let him win so she doubled her efforts, changing her rhythm to combine into a grinding bounce that only spurred Logan on.

It took mere moments for the swell of pleasure to build and crest. Jackie cried out his name as her orgasm hit her. She was dimly aware of his shout somewhere in the distance, but she knew he had come at the same time.

She slowed her rocking, enjoying the aftershocks her movement created.

"I think that was a draw," he grumbled, dragging her down to kiss her languidly. "I think we need to do it again just to be sure."

"Later." She laughed and slipped off him to lay cradled against his side. "Preferably once we can move again." When he turned to his side to face her with a hopeful grin on his face she shook her head. "After the wedding."

"Okay, okay." He relented. "It's going to be torture to get through the day. You know that, right?"

Of course, wasn't she going to suffer the same thing? "I'm sure we'll both survive."

He mumbled something that sounded negative, but he wound his arms around her. "This feels good, doesn't it? It feels right."

It did. "Yes."

His laughed rumbled through them both. "I'm glad you think so too." Logan lifted his gaze to look her in the eyes. "I want things to work out for us, this time."

"So do I." They still had so much to talk about. But they had time. Their relationship had shifted into something more, and she wanted to believe that it would all come together. "We should think about getting ready."

"Thinking about it is about all I'm capable of at the moment."

Laughing, she clambered off the bed. "I'm serious. We're in the wedding. We can't let them down."

He let out a gusty sigh and followed suit. "I'll get the shower started."

She smiled just as she got a text alert on her phone. "It's probably Caroline reminding me of the time. I'll meet you in there."

Logan gave her a peck. "I'm coming to find you if you're not in there in five minutes."

Nodding, she tapped her screen and read. "It might take a bit longer, she needs to talk to me about something urgently. She's on her way here now."

Logan rolled his eyes. "She's such a drama queen."

"Just let me talk to her. She probably just needs to get out some last-minute jitters."

He grazed her lips with his. "I'm kidding. It's a big step she's about to make. Take your time."

Glad he understood, she smiled. "See you in there."

He winked and disappeared into the bathroom.

Jackie grabbed a robe and slung it around herself moments before there was a soft knock on the door.

She opened it a crack to find Caroline, paler than usual, on the other side.

"What's wrong?" Jackie grabbed her friend's arm and dragged her inside. "Are you stressed about the wedding again?"

She shook her head as she walked into the room and looked around. Her eyes widened at the sight of the massage table and the disarray of the bed. "What the hell have you two— You know what? Never mind. I don't want to know. Is Logan here?"

Jackie nodded her head toward the bathroom. "He's in the shower."

Caroline relaxed a tiny bit, but tensed again immediately when she looked Jackie directly in the eyes. "I have something to tell you and you're not going to like it."

"What is it?"

She linked arms with Jackie and dragged her out to the balcony. She stared out into the distant water for a long moment.

Jackie's heart lurched the moment her friend had said she had something important to tell her. Now it was galloping in her chest as she waited. "Caroline. You're freaking me out."

Turning her gaze back to Jackie, Caroline took a deep breath. "Charles told me that Logan came to him about a day ago with some concerns about you wanting advice on how to break things off."

Her heart froze. Jackie had to forcibly inhale and exhale a couple of times to jump start her lungs. "He must be mistaken."

"I'm sorry, Jackie. Charles said there was no way to misconstrue what was going on. He came down to breakfast, which was out of the ordinary and what brought up the conversation in the first place. He cornered Charles trying to figure out what to do about you. How to make it clear that it was just…sex between you two."

The world dropped out from under Jackie. She gripped the railing as she tried to make sense of everything Caroline said.

After all the things that had happened between them. All the things they'd both said… Charles had to have gotten things wrong. Or Caroline had it all turned around. She never like Logan to begin with…

And now she was rationalizing.

She needed a moment to get her head together. If he was just using her why would he say all those things? Did he get his kicks out of hurting her? Was she just going to let him do it again?

After yesterday, she wanted to believe that their relationship had changed, she even thought that what they had this time around might have been stronger than before.

Jackie pushed off the railing and stomped back inside.

"What are you doing?"

"What do you think? I'm going to ask him about it."

"Are you sure that's a good idea?"

Jackie slowed a little. Was it? Probably not, especially not before something as huge and public as her friend's wedding.

"I don't want to sound like a selfish bitch, but I'd rather not have one of my bridesmaids strangling a groomsman as they walk down the aisle."

"That could happen whether or not I talk to him."

"Do you think you can hold off on both until after the ceremony?"

They would talk about things after the wedding. She'd make sure of it. Jackie knocked on the bathroom door, unwilling to open it and see him. "Logan? I'm going to head back to my suite and get ready. I'll see you at the wedding."

The water stopped immediately and he opened the door, dripping wet with a towel haphazardly slung around his hips.

She hated that he looked so enticing.

"Is everything all right?"

Nodding, she choked back the questions. The bile.

"Hey." He stepped out as he secured the towel around himself. "What's the matter?"

When he would have touched her, Jackie lurched backward. "I just have to go."

He held her gaze for a moment before it darted to Caroline and back. "Caroline. Can you excuse us for a minute?"

She shook her head reflexively. "We're on a tight schedule."

Logan's expression shuttered. "Right. I guess I'll see you at the ceremony."

He grasped Jackie's hand as she turned, drawing her gaze up to meet his. "Jackie…"

She pulled her hand from his. "I'll see you in a little while."

Logan watched the door close behind the two women, completely confused over what had just happened. Jackie seemed to have completely shut him out in the span of a conversation with Caroline.

What the hell had the woman said to cause such a reaction?

Stomach in knots, he dried himself off hurriedly. There was still a couple of hours left until the wedding and he hadn't planned anything more than getting dressed and turning up. Jackie's regimen was sure to be a bit more complicated than that.

That would hardly stress her out as much as she appeared to be. Did Caroline bring bad news? Had someone shown up and that's what concerned her? Had someone said something?

He fought the overwhelming urge to dash down the hall after her and find out just what was going on.

Instead he walked out onto the balcony and dropped onto the lounger, uncaring of his nude state. All he wanted to know was what was going through Jackie's mind. He had no clue how it worked, and worst of all, Caroline seemed to know exactly what to say to get Jackie to do whatever she wanted.

What was going on?

It had to be something Caroline had done or said. Jackie had been pale and fighting back tears. Of course she would be upset. She was about to be in a wedding and that last thing she would want to do was look terrible and draw more attention to herself. That didn't stop him from wanting to wipe that pain away, however.

Once again, he would give her the chance to come to him. He wasn't sure how much longer he could continue to do so. His nature was to meet obstacles head on. He knew Jackie didn't like confrontation and had turned avoidance into an art form. It was just so hard to sit by and let things hurt her if there was a possibility he could help.

But Jackie was a grown woman and she knew what was best for herself.

Even if he thought he knew better.

Tiring of all the pointless speculation, he got up and dove into the pool. Maybe he would be able to burn off the anxiety.

* * * *

For the next hour, he stayed in the water swimming laps and thinking things over. He knew he had to get ready, but Logan could barely bring himself to care how he looked. The people he was going to be paraded in front of had no bearing on him. He didn't know anyone beside Jackie and the bride and groom. And besides Jackie, he didn't give a damn about what anyone thought about him.

For her sake, he slowed down and took some care in his appearance. If they were to be walking down the aisle together, he wanted to make an effort for Jackie.

Logan took a little time to primp, not that it was something he knew much about. He had the tux, the shoes, a search through the bathroom yielded some hair products. He used a bit of wax to tame his hair and stared at himself. Not much of a difference, but he looked good, if he did say so himself.

He got to the lobby to meet up with the groomsmen with nearly fifty minutes to spare.

Charles was already there, a little wide-eyed and pale, but happy. Several groomsmen were also waiting, all resplendent in their tuxes.

"Hey." Logan clapped the man on the shoulder. "Feeling good?"

"Like I'm about to vomit, but that's to be expected, right?"

Logan laughed. "Sure, why not? We stood in for you two when you missed the rehearsal yesterday."

"Thanks for that." Charles swallowed audibly. "I was surprised to hear you and Jackie did that together."

"Why is that?"

"Because of what you said the other day at breakfast. The last thing I thought you'd want to do was something like that with a woman you didn't want to lead on."

A ball of ice formed in Logan's gut. "You didn't happen to mention that conversation to Caroline, did you?"

"Shouldn't I have?" He took one look at Logan and sighed. "Sorry. I guess I wasn't thinking. With everything going on... I screwed something up, didn't I?"

Logan barely heard the man. Of course, Caroline would have heard that and gone straight to Jackie with it. No wonder she was in such a hurry to get out of there.

Logan dragged his hands through his hair. "Where are the women getting ready?"

"They've ensconced themselves in Caroline's room."

"Where is it? What number?"

Charles checked his watch and shook his head. "They're probably on their way now."

He wasn't about to give in that easily. "Which way are they coming from?"

The coordinator chose that moment to appear. Her chirpy attitude immediately cut Logan to the quick. She quickly got Charles out of the way and arranged the men in a neat little line as she reminded everyone of the routine they were about to exercise.

Logan let himself get pushed into line, taking solace in the fact that Jackie would soon be next to him and he could at least try to explain himself.

Instead, as the music started and the couples in front of him started to walk down onto the beach, he found himself standing next to a petite redhead he vaguely remembered seeing at the meals and the rehearsal.

"Where's Jackie?"

"There's been a change of plans." She linked her arm firmly through his and put a bright smile on her face.

As much as he wanted to drag her back and find Jackie, he knew she wouldn't appreciate him throwing everything off just to find her. So Logan gritted his teeth and carried on.

He stood silently at the altar, watching as Jackie made her way down the aisle on the arm of one of the dickheads who had commented on how hot she was that morning at breakfast. Logan bet he'd jumped at the chance of walking with Jackie.

Watching them like a hawk, Logan stared at Jackie. She outshone the bride in the delicate peach-colored dress. They might have all looked like the same doll with varying hair colors the way Caroline had them lined up in identical dresses, with their hair in loose buns, but Jackie definitely stood out from the others. He wanted to brush his hand on the skin exposed at her nape, knowing how soft and smooth it would be. Her eyes were a bit pink and had a haunted quality to them, and her skin was a bit pale. Even the expertly applied makeup couldn't hide that. Still, she was easily the most beautiful woman he'd ever seen.

She refused to turn her gaze toward him as she approached with the forced smile on her lips. Jackie looked everywhere but at him. She joined the others to stand stiffly in the line.

As all eyes turned to watch Caroline, Logan's attention stayed riveted to Jackie. He needed to set things straight between them. Get everything out in the open.

The ceremony went smoothly, at least as far as he could tell. He was just glad he didn't have to do anything more than stand there, because all he could do was stare at Jackie and try to will her to meet his gaze. As if a simple look could fix everything.

She refused to. There were a few moments when he had been sure she was about to burst into tears. Jackie would exert her superhuman control over her emotions and rein it in to look serene again. Though he could see from the turmoil in her eyes that she was anything but.

The rest of the formalities were agonizing to get through. Whoever invented a receiving line needed to be shot. Then there were the photos. *So. Many. Photos.* To be so close to Jackie and yet have her pretend like he wasn't even there was aggravating. Trying to keep his expression placid instead of as if he was about to kill someone wasn't easy.

The longer he had to endure the treatment the angrier he became. His temper wasn't going to hold out for much longer.

They went from photos directly to the reception. And finally a chance to talk to Jackie.

He sat at the table ignoring the redhead's attempts at chitchat. He took note when both Jackie and Caroline had disappeared, that wasn't really surprising. But when Caroline reappeared alone, alarms bells pealed in his mind.

Logan walked straight over to Caroline. "Where's Jackie?"

She glared at him and waved him away dismissively. "What do you care?"

"You have no idea what you did, Caroline." Because he wanted to shake her, he took a half step back. "I know you hate me and think I'm beneath her, but did you really have to ruin our relationship again?"

She jabbed him in the chest. "You did that yourself last time. Why do you think I didn't want her getting involved with you again? It took her forever to get back on her feet after her last round with you."

"What are you talking about?"

"You took off on Jackie, you asshole!" she snarled. "You just walked out on her and left her there—alone!"

Logan dragged her aside, away from eyes that were beginning to turn their way. "Is that what she told you? That *I* walked out on *her*?"

Caroline stepped out of his grip to jab an accusing finger at him. "Everyone knows what you did to her.

Why do you think everyone points and stares at her? She's the fallen Pennington. The poor little rich girl who had abandoned her life for a man who didn't want her. The tale is all but legendary."

Logan felt as though his head was going to explode. Clenching and unclenching his hands in his hair, he struggled to understand what he was being told. "What?"

Caroline narrowed her gaze at him. "As if you don't know. And now you're about to do the same thing once more. I'm not letting you hurt my friend again."

He fought to calm his breathing, his voice. "Will you just explain what you're talking about? What everyone, apparently, has been talking about?"

She glared at him as if he was an idiot. "They love to talk about the fact that Jackie dropped everything to be with some poor boy. She told her parents off and walked out of their lives, only he wasn't man enough to be there for her. *You* weren't man enough to be there for her. Or maybe you realized that what you wanted wasn't her, but her money. And without that, she wasn't worth your time."

Logan felt as though he had been kicked in the gut by a horse. *That* was what everyone was whispering about? Insane rumors and speculation about what had happened to Jackie when they were younger? What Caroline had said turned his stomach until he was sure he was going to be sick. Was that what Jackie thought of him? What she thought he did?

Jesus.

"Where did she go?" His phone rang, but after a negligent glance at the screen, he dismissed the call.

She narrowed her eyes, glancing at him suspiciously to his phone then back to him. "I'm not tell you anything, Logan."

He raked his hands through his hair. "Caroline. Trust me when I say you have things so very wrong. I need to talk to Jackie."

She stared at him for a long moment. While she did his phone went off again. "Something you need to get?"

He swiped the screen angrily. "No."

In that time, Charles found them and closed his arm around his new wife's shoulders. "Everything okay?"

Not at all.

Head reeling Logan had to concentrate to stay standing up. "Please. I have to talk to Jackie. Just tell me where she is."

Caroline's expression had changed from condemnation to confusion to pale realization. "You had no idea, did you?"

He shook his head as he still tried to process the information. Jackie had turned her back on her life for him? And everyone thought he had walked out on her as well? She had been alone all this time? Struggling? He should have been there with her. He could have been there with her if he hadn't have been so stupid. Each thought was a bomb exploding in his head.

"Then what the hell happened, Logan?" Caroline put a hesitant hand on his shoulder but quickly took it away again when he glared at her.

He didn't want to talk to anyone but Jackie. "Just tell me where she is. This is between me and her."

"I helped her pack and got her in a cab." Caroline held up her hands helplessly. "Jackie didn't want to give you the chance to hurt her again. She's on her way to the airport. She's headed home."

Swearing under his breath, he turned and ran for the lobby. Logan called ahead and demanded that a cab be waiting for him. As he dashed outside, a cab pulled up. Without hesitation, he jumped into the back. "Airport.

There's an extra two hundred dollars in it for you if you get me there in twenty minutes."

* * * *

Jackie walked into the air-conditioned airport and felt suffocated. She knew she was freaking out. It was her instinct to run. To protect herself before he could hurt her again. But was hurting herself first the answer?

Probably not.

She just needed time to think. The trip to the airport was long enough to figure out that what she felt for Logan wasn't going to go away. Jackie felt betrayed and angry and confused. But the underlying love was there. And that's what hurt. She loved him. Again? Still? She loved him and he had used that for what? As a game? Did he think she was just a toy to play with and discard when he was done with her?

Jackie didn't want to believe it. She couldn't. The way he had been — they had been — over the past few days... It had been bliss. It felt so real.

Could she have imagined it all? Maybe the romance of the location had been at fault? Could she have been so starved for someone that made her feel the way Logan had in the past that she had fooled herself in believing a mirage?

Jackie sighed. She could go around in circles in her mind all day long.

She stared at the counters and approached them slowly. Running now...it would make her a coward. She'd prided herself on being strong and building her life up from nothing. Wouldn't this just prove she hadn't changed at all from the girl who relied her parents for everything?

She turned away and started walking.

What she needed was time to think.

Wandering around an airport probably wasn't the smartest place to do it, but she was there now.

She pulled the handle out of the suitcase and dragged it long behind her.

* * * *

The ride to the airport was the longest trip he'd ever had to endure. Of all the things he thought might have happened to Jackie after they had parted ways, he'd never imagined she had gone off on her own.

Anger boiled over at himself for being so bullheaded that he never tried to look for her. At her parents for lying to him and for letting her leave. And at Jackie herself for not telling him.

He spent the entire trip seething that it wasn't until he arrived at the airport that he realized that he had no idea where Jackie had gone. He knew nothing about her life now.

That didn't stop him from running into the terminal and searching up and down to find her. He received some strange looks and some inviting smiles before he realized he was chasing Jackie down in a tuxedo.

Logan didn't care how ridiculous he came across. He pulled out his phone again and called Charles, hoping that he'd brought his phone with him to the reception.

He only had to wait a few seconds before when he was rewarded with Charles' voice.

"Have you found her?"

"No. I have no idea where to even start."

Logan could hear Charles asking Caroline before he answered. "You want the British Airways flight to London Gatwick."

"Thanks."

"Good luck."

Logan hung up and looked for any display that would help him as he ran.

Eventually, he identified the gate and hoped he wasn't too late to catch her before she got past security.

Logan was sure he caught a glimpse of her not too far ahead of him and he turned his jog into a sprint to catch up with her. "Jackie!"

She stiffened, but continued to walk.

Knowing that he'd found her, the ache in his chest loosened a little. At least she hadn't gotten on a plane.

When he dodged all the people between him and Jackie he stepped into her path. "Jackie."

She stepped around him. "I don't want to hear it, Logan."

He spun and kept up with her. "Jackie, *please*. You have to hear me out. We need to talk. About everything."

She doggedly kept her pace. "What is there to say? You were just using me. Just like I was using you."

"That might have been what you were doing. Maybe even how it started for me in the beginning, but not anymore."

"How could anything have possibly changed in that short a time? You and I both know that kind of thing only exists in fairy tales."

Logan stepped in front of her again. "Because I never stopped loving you."

She paused for a moment. "Liar."

"I swear. You're the only woman I've ever loved."

Jackie began to tremble then. "Then why did you do it? Why did you leave me?"

Fat tears rolled down her cheeks, and Logan's heart cracked a little. He pried the luggage from her hand before grasping it firmly in his own then pulled her aside.

An airport was hardly the place for this conversation, but it was where it was going to happen. He found a spot that was somewhat secluded and sat her on top of her suitcase.

"I didn't know that was what I did." Logan got down on his knees in front of her so he was level with her eyes. "Your dad came out and told me *you* didn't want *me*. That I could wait out there for the rest of my life but you would never want someone like me. That I would never be good enough for you and you had finally realized it."

She stared at him. "What? How could you believe that?"

"While I waited for you, he found me and gave me a message he said was from you." He sighed. "I was hidden where I usually waited for you and figured the only way he found me was because you had told him."

Jackie took a hiccupping breath. "All I told him and my mother was that I was leaving to be with you. I had a terrible fight with them and gathered what I could carry to meet you. Only you weren't there."

His stomach clutched as he remembered the pain he'd gone through as he'd stood in the darkness, trying to comprehend that the woman he loved hadn't wanted him. "I had waited a while, hoping that you would magically appear to at least tell me to my face that you didn't want me."

"How could I not want you? I had given up everything to be with you."

"And you couldn't just walk back in after what had been said." He closed his hands around hers. "I'm so sorry, Jackie. I should have had more faith in you."

"Yeah, you should have."

"Please come back to the resort. We have a lot to talk about." He had so much to make up for.

It was surreal, what Logan was saying, and yet she could absolutely believe that her parents had been so meddlesome. At the time Logan was unsure of himself. It would have taken a master manipulator like her father no time to find his weakness and exploit it. In his case, Logan's feelings of inadequacy had been his Achilles' heel.

But he was right, he should have had more faith in her. In their love.

One more day couldn't hurt. She hadn't planned to leave until the next day anyway. She wanted things to finally be out in the open between them too.

Jackie nodded.

Logan wasted no time in getting her on her feet and whisking her back through the airport. He fired off a series of texts then called for a cab. While they waited, he refused to let her or her suitcase go.

So when a limo pulled up, Jackie was mildly surprised.

"I wanted us to get back there in style."

Jackie watched as he handed the suitcase over to the driver. He opened the door for and held his hand out to her. "Princess."

She laughed a little, as she took his hand and climbed in.

Logan followed close behind and slid in to sit next to her. He stared her in the eyes and she could see he had so much to say.

"I don't know where to begin." He brushed a stray strand of hair from her face. "But if you give me the chance, I'll spend the rest of my life making it up to you."

It was a sweet sentiment. "I don't want that."

Logan dropped his hand and shifted backward. "I see."

Jackie shook her head. "I don't think that you do." She took his hands and pulled him close. "I don't want you to feel as if you owe me. If we're going to do this, I want us going ahead as equals."

A smile slowly spread over his mouth. "Does this mean you want to try to make things work?"

"We have a lot to discuss, but I think we could." This time around they were wiser, stronger. They could be happy.

His phone buzzed, but he swiped the screen and dropped it onto the seat next to them. "How about we start with where you went afterward?"

Jackie took a deep breath. "Needless to say I was completely freaked out. I tried to find you, but you had all but disappeared." She had gone to his dorm room hoping to find him, but he hadn't come back.

He tightened his arms around her. "Hurting from your rejection, I took off for a while."

She could still feel the pain in her chest that she felt when she realized he wasn't coming back. She'd lain on the bed they had shared on so many occasions contemplating her future. "When you never came back, I took stock of my situation. Moved to a smaller school and sold what I had taken with me to afford tuition when I went into education."

Logan smiled wonderingly at her. "You teach?"

"I'm a primary school teacher." A fact she was proud of.

"That's amazing. I bet you're great at that."

"I enjoy it very much. And the kids seem to like me and appear to learn, so I guess I'm a success."

"I knew you'd be great at whatever you ended up doing. But working with kids sounds like it's a perfect fit."

Nodding, she smiled. "I love what I do."

"I'm glad." Logan stared at her a long while. "You're incredible. Not many people could do what you did."

"It was hard, I'm not going to lie. But I think I became stronger for it." She laughed softly. "I couldn't have done it—wouldn't have—if things hadn't turned out the way they did."

"I'm still responsible," he grumbled. "I hate that you had to suffer so much on your own when I could have easily been there to help. If not with money than at least emotionally."

She shrugged. "We can't change that now."

"But we can change where things are going." He cupped her cheeks. "I know what Caroline told you I said to Charles, but they both had it completely wrong." Touching his nose to hers, he continued, "I had gone down to breakfast thinking I could get information from Charles about why people always seemed to be talking about you. It was pissing me off, and you wouldn't talk about it. All I knew was that I had to do something about it. But he assumed that we'd hooked up and that it was getting messy and gave me advice. Which turned out to be what you were telling me, that you didn't want to take things further. I came out of that conversation wanting to convince you that I was worth taking a chance on."

She sighed. "But, of course, you never told him any of that and just let him continue thinking what he wanted."

He shrugged. "Since when do I ever feel the need to explain myself to others?"

Typical Logan.

"So when did you decide things had changed between us?"

He smiled and without a beat he replied, "At the pool. The first night."

Jackie flushed at the memory of him bringing her to an embarrassingly easy orgasm with just his fingers in the pool.

"So pretty much right away."

He chuckled. "Yeah, though I did my best to try and twist it around in my head to ignore the fact that seeing you again knocked me for a loop. I didn't want to admit it, but everything came rushing back. *Everything*."

The exact same thing had happened to her once she'd gotten over the shock of seeing him again.

"So where did you go...after?"

"I actually went to work. I was going to tell you that night that I had been accepted at a tech firm. They had a few openings internationally. Originally, I had taken a position in London, but after what I thought had happened, I took the one in Copenhagen."

She gazed at him in awe. He had come so far from the guy she had once known.

"While I was there I started developing my own software on my down time and the rest is history."

"I'm proud of you. I knew you would make it."

"Thanks." He seemed to think for a little bit. "I guess you're right that things worked out the way they did because of what happened."

Jackie leaned against him. It felt so good to be with him and to speak so openly about everything.

His phone went off again, and they both looked.

Logan scowled and impatiently swiped the screen, rejecting the call.

"Someone seems pretty determined to get you. Maybe you should answer."

"It's nothing…" He sighed when she stared at him waiting for an explanation. "It's the owner of another hotel chain that's interested in using my software. I was supposed to be meeting with him this evening."

Jackie could believe what she was hearing. "You gave up work commitments to come for me?"

"In a heartbeat." He kissed her. "You're the most important thing in my life."

Tears welled in her eyes as her heart swelled at his declaration.

Logan ran his finger down her cheek. "Do you think you can ever forgive me?"

"If you can forgive me hating you all these years."

Logan swept in close, cradling her head for a soft kiss full of hope and promise. It slowly grew deeper. He pressed closer, dragging her under him she he could look her in the eyes.

Smiling up at him, Jackie inched her hand up his chest. "We've never had sex in a limo, you know."

"Another place to cross off the list?" He helped her unbutton his shirt.

Jackie loved the feel of his solid chest under her fingers. He was so hard and warm. She wanted to feel his skin against hers — needed to reassert her claim over him, to reaffirm their connection.

She ran her hands over the muscles of his abdomen to slide along the waistband of his trousers. Winding her legs around his, she pressed herself against him. It wasn't long before his arousal made itself known.

She ran her fingers lightly over him, grazing the head of his erection with teasing strokes. When he groaned impatiently and tugged her in for a biting kiss, she went to work on the fastening of his trousers, shoving them and his boxers down over his hips, freeing his erection.

Closing her hand around him, she reveled in the feel of him, hard and smooth, in her hand. She had that power over him. As much as he turned her on, she did the same to him. That she could bring Logan to his knees was both humbling and potent.

He skimmed his hand up her leg to slip between them, seeking her core. She was already wet and ready for him as he teased her with sure fingers. Jackie let out a little squeal when Logan went straight for her clit. He drove two fingers into her, rubbing the swollen bundle of nerves with broad strokes of his thumb.

"As happy as I would be to feel you come around my fingers, I would rather be inside you when it hits you. I want to feel every pulse and flutter and know I did that. That I made you climax."

"Anything." And Jackie meant it. She would do anything for him and let him do anything to her. The knowledge that he would never do a thing to hurt her made the word easy to say.

He groaned when she punctuated her words with a squeeze. "I can't wait."

With a flip, he twisted her over, spreading her under him. He quickly took care of protection. Pushing her skirt up and tearing aside her panties, Logan thrust into Jackie all the way to the hilt.

The pleasure from that one move rocketed through her, radiating through her body and down her limbs to tingle in her fingers and toes.

She raked his shoulders. "More."

Logan immediately increased the speed and power. It was going to be hard and fast, and Jackie wouldn't have it any other way. His thrusts were deep, satisfying, amazing. Jackie arched to meet each one, building the pleasure, the pressure.

Logan gripped one leg under her knee and pushed it upward, changing the angle and allowing him to thrust even deeper.

Jackie held his gaze as he strained over her. The feel of him so deep inside her was awe-inspiring.

Her climb to orgasm was fast — too fast.

Jackie gently pushed him back. She wanted to savor the moment. "Let me on top."

His thrusts were slow and penetrating before he relented. Logan sat back, keeping hold of her. For a moment, as he shifted inside her, Jackie almost lost it. She sat motionless on him for a bit while she fought the impending tsunami of sensation.

"Something wrong?" Logan brushed her hair out of her face and cupped her cheeks to peer into her eyes.

She sighed happily as she rocked. "I'm just trying to make it last."

He chuckled, gripping her hips in his hands and helping her move. "We've got the rest of our lives, princess."

That was all it took.

Bright spots appeared in her vision just an instant before her orgasm caught her off guard and slammed into her, knocking her breath from her lungs.

Logan joined her seconds later, clinging to her as he fought to regain his breath.

Jackie held him, loving the closeness she felt with him at that moment. What was there between them wasn't going to go away.

* * * *

The instant they walked back into the hotel, they were caught up in a whirlwind. A darkly handsome man stood at the reception desk having a hushed argument with the receptionist there. The man quailed, shook his head helplessly. His eyes widened when he spotted Logan. He pointed and both men turned to look directly at him.

"Give me a second, will you, Jackie?" He kissed her cheek and started walking over to the men. Just as he was about to relinquish her hand, he stopped. "Actually, come with me."

Jackie held his hand and followed. "Who is he?"

"Gabriel Sosa, quality assurance for Totally Five Star. I'm betting he's here because of how the security feed's been glitching."

Jackie slowed him down. "Logan, he'll be livid if he finds out what you've been doing."

"Just let me handle it." He squeezed her hand. "It'll be fine."

She wasn't so sure.

"Logan. Good to see you."

"Good to see you too, Gabriel." He proudly put his arm around Jackie. "This is Jacqueline Pennington. Jackie, Gabriel Sosa."

Gabriel took her hand and kissed the back of it, giving her a charming smile. "A pleasure."

Jackie's her cheeks heated up at the contact. His accent was charming as well. Spanish was her guess. "Nice to meet you."

"Your man here is a genius."

She grinned and jostled Logan. "I like to think so."

"I hope you'll forgive us speaking about business for a moment."

Jackie shook her head with a shrug. "No problem."

Nestling further under Logan's arm, she anxiously listened.

"I'm just on one of my stops. I like to check in unannounced to see how things are going. I'm pleased to say that things here are running almost effortlessly. I wanted to thank you for staying around, Logan. I've been told the cameras have been acting up, but you've been right there to sort them out every time."

Logan smiled, and his muscles relaxed slightly under her fingers. "No thanks are needed. I'm just glad that the system is up and running."

Gabriel turned to Jackie, nodding apologetically. "I've taken up enough of your evening." He kissed her hand again. "I hope you have a good night."

Logan shook his hand. "I'm sure we will."

He jostled her when they were out of earshot. "You're blushing."

"I was panicked." She fought the urge to fan her cheeks. "He's very handsome."

"Oh, yeah?"

"But not as handsome as you," she soothed.

Logan swatted her ass with a laugh. "Nice save."

Her spirits were high as they walked through the hotel. They avoided everything to do with the wedding and headed straight into the building. When they arrived at his suite, Logan swiped his card and held the door open for her.

Jackie gasped as she walked in. The room had been filled with exotic flowers and candles. Out on the balcony, a table had been set up with two chairs, more candles...

"This is beautiful."

"I'm glad you think so." He dropped her suitcase on the floor and urged her toward the balcony.

"I suppose that's what the texts were about." She smiled up at him. "You know, every time we've been together you've being doing stuff on your phone."

"Okay... In the spirit of full disclosure." Logan paused.

"Well?"

"I've been using the hotel cameras to find you." He put up his hands when her eyes bugged. "Only when I couldn't find you or needed to talk to you. And…"

"There's more?"

"I kind of ensured our privacy when we were naked in public."

All at once, she felt both violated and wonderfully taken care of. "What happens if they find out what you've been doing?"

"Let me worry about that." Logan pulled out her chair for her. "Right now we're going to enjoy dinner."

She sat. "How do you expect me not to worry? It's your name on the line and you did it to be with me."

Leaning over the table, he gave her a lingering kiss. "I would risk a hell of a lot more than that to be with you, Jackie."

He sat back and waved at the table. "*Bon appétit.*"

Heart fluttering, she eyed what was waiting for them. A huge lobster, sautéed vegetables, a salad, and a bottle of chardonnay sat ready to be shared.

"When we were younger, this was the meal I wanted to be able to give you whenever you wanted."

"I mentioned it one time." Jackie laughed. It had been in passing one night when he asked what her family had had for dinner that weekend. She had answered honestly and never thought any more about it. Obviously Logan had. "This is amazing."

"Also." He revealed a tray he had hidden next to him. "I have this as well." He lifted the concealing dome to show her a vanilla cheesecake.

Her favorite dessert. "You remembered."

"Of course I did."

Tears welled up in her eyes. "You did all this for me, what's in it for you?"

"I got you." Logan paused and looked her in the eyes holding her gaze.

Jackie knew there was no going back once she saw Logan again. Once they'd made love. There was no man on earth more fitting for her than Logan.

"You do."

He relaxed in his seat and smiled. "You're letting your food get cold." Before she could dig in, he picked up a piece of the lobster in his fingers and dipped it in the butter before offering it to her.

Jackie opened her mouth and let him slip it in between her lips. Butter dribbled down her chin.

"Let me get that." Logan delicately kissed it from her skin.

It was succulent, sweet and delicate. Delicious. It was a shame that he wasn't enjoying it as well.

"But what about you? Aren't you hungry?" Jackie copied his move and slipped a bit of the lobster into his mouth, but made sure to be as sloppy as possible in getting it to her goal.

When his tongue darted out reflexively to collect the stray butter, she swooped in. The combined flavors were even better than the meal alone.

Jackie licked his lips before sitting back again.

"I love you, Jackie. I need you to know that."

And she did. Jackie could see it shining at her through his eyes. She sensed it coming off him in waves. "I know. I love you too. So much."

He grinned. Logan ran his hands up her thighs. "Traditionally, a declaration of love would be celebrated physically."

Laughing, she arched her eyebrows at him. "Really? I've never heard that."

"No? I guess I'll have to teach you all about it." Logan stood and extended his hand.

She took it and let him lead her to the balcony. "Please do."

Logan wound his arms around her and rocked them to an imaginary beat. "Well, when two people love each other, they tend to get naked a lot." He tugged down the zipper at the back of her dress.

Jackie let it slip down to fall at their feet as she went to work on his shirt. "Do they? And what do they do without their clothes?"

She shrugged out of his shirt and helped her with the fastening on his trousers. "Whatever comes naturally, of course."

"I see. What happens if one of them is a bit shy?"

"Then the other does their best to ease their anxiety." He stepped back to look at her.

Standing in the glow of the candles in her lingerie under his scrutiny, Jackie had never felt more relaxed and happy. He ran his hands up her sides to twine them behind her back and pull her close.

"You are beautiful," he whispered. "And smart and so strong. I don't know how I got so lucky to find you again."

She rested her cheek against his chest to listen to the strong beat of his heart. "We both lucked out."

Logan lowered his head to capture her mouth with his. "Promise me we'll never let anything come between us again."

She cupped his cheek. "I swear. Nothing and no one."

With a grin, Logan picked her up and carried her back into the room.

He peeled away her bra and panties slowly, reverently, treating each bit of skin he revealed with a kiss and a caress. Jackie arched under him, luxuriating in every sensation that he coaxed out of her. His touched feathered over her skin sensitizing it incredibly despite him barely making contact. He kissed his way up her leg, stopping to kiss her belly, her breasts, to pin her to the bed with his body. The feel of him pressed against her sparked more heat.

The liquid ache low in her belly grew more insistent as he continued to languidly explore her body. Logan drove her crazy, building the tension to a fever pitch without breaking a sweat. Jackie wasn't going to lie back and just be a spectator.

Dragging a hand down over his chest, she stopped to close her hand around his arousal while she slid her other hand up his back and into his hair to pull him in for a kiss.

Undulating against him, she grinned when Logan groaned against her lips. He grabbed a condom and slipped it on an instant before burying himself inside her.

The pace he set was slow and deep and oh so satisfying. Every vein on his erection dragged against her, creating the most incredible friction. Every hitch of his hips bumped her clit, sending sparks of pleasure shooting through her.

When her orgasm exploded, Jackie clutched Logan to her as he plunged into her and came with a groan.

Still trembling from the aftershocks, he rolled them both to their sides so he could gaze into her eyes.

Jackie knew nothing would keep them apart again.

Epilogue

One year later

Jackie held Logan's hand as they walked into the hotel lobby. For her Christmas vacation, as a surprise, he'd whisked her away with him on a business trip to Vienna.

She stared at the interior of the hotel in awe. Over the past year, Logan had taken her to a string of Totally Five Star Hotels and none had ceased to amaze her. Each one seemed to top the last in opulence and pure decadence.

"What do you think?"

She stepped up to the lavishly decorated tree and stared at the glittering ornaments. "It's incredible."

"I thought you might like it here."

He knew her so well.

The truth was, she liked being wherever he was, and he seemed to enjoy being with her. Knowing how important her job was to her, Logan had come to visit her at her tiny house as often as he could. Over the past couple of months, he'd shown up more frequently and finally admitted that he'd been scouting the area for a place for them both so that she wouldn't have to quit her job.

He showed her a selection before they'd found the perfect home in a penthouse apartment twice the size of her house that was only a short commute to work. On the night she moved in, Logan had proposed with a massive diamond ring and Jackie hadn't even had to think about it. Everything had just fallen blissfully into place.

"I'll get us checked in." He pecked her on the cheek before stepping away.

Jackie nodded. She wanted to get a good look at the lobby. Each hotel was fantastically unique and she loved to see the differences. What she never got tired of was seeing how the local flair colored the décor. In the tropics it was all about the exotic flowers and ornately carved woodwork. In Europe the designs were all about gleaming stonework and Old World opulence. Each time she walked into one of the hotels, she found a new favorite. She couldn't wait to visit ones in the Far East or South America. She could only imagine how magnificent they would be.

They certainly hadn't skimped on decorations. The scent of fresh pine and holly wafted through the air, mingling with cinnamon and the Totally Five Star signature scent. It was muted, but it gave the ambience another level of sophistication.

She wandered through, admiring the décor. The dark wood furniture that graced the waiting area gleamed. The plush carpet muffled her steps as she explored the beautifully decorated space. Jackie circled the tree again, marveling at the sheer size of it. How had they brought it in? She had to walk almost to the wall to see a hint of the glittering golden star at the top. It grazed the uppermost part of the glass dome overhead.

Jackie ran her fingers over the greenery that was wound around the walls and decorated the tables. It was all real. The upkeep must have been a nightmare.

"All set." Logan wound an arm around her waist, leading her away from the desk.

Jackie leaned into him with a smile as they made their way back through the lobby. Nothing could be more perfect in that moment.

"Jacqueline?"

Jackie hesitantly turned toward the startled voice and froze. She barely managed to choke out, "Mum. Dad."

Logan tensed next to her.

She stared numbly at her parents. They looked the same as she remembered them, though perhaps a little grayer. Well-dressed and poised, they could have been any wealthy couple staying at the luxurious hotel. They fit the ambiance, as if by design. But to Jackie they were little more than strangers staring at them with wide-eyed surprise.

Unsure of what she was supposed to do in this situation, Jackie stood anchored to Logan's side, waiting for them to start the conversation.

Logan held her tightly, lending her his strength, standing tense and silent as if he understood what was going through her mind. He would follow her lead and back up whatever choice she made.

"It's lovely to see you again." Her mother took a half step forward, but stopped, clearly unsure of what to do as well.

Jackie forced a tight smile as her father eyed Logan up and down.

She saw the grudging admiration as her father sized them up and felt a surge of pride as her father grumbled, "You've certainly come up in the world."

"I'm sorry to disappoint you." Logan's arm tightened around Jackie. "Now if you'll excuse us."

"Wait." Her mother reached out to snare her hand, pausing a moment when she noticed the huge diamond sparkling there, rivaling the ones she wore. "Would you both have dinner with us? We're here for the next few days. If you're willing, I hear the hotel has several excellent restaurants."

"We'll see." Jackie smiled up at Logan who still looked grim. "We have a busy week." In the spirit of the season, Jackie gave her mother, then her father, brief hugs. "Merry Christmas."

As they walked away, Logan hugged her close. "I'm sorry. If I'd known they were here…"

"What? You'd have left me at home? Gotten them kicked out?" She leaned her head against his shoulder. "It's okay. Really. It was bound to happen sooner or later." With the amount of traveling they'd done lately and the wanderlust her parents had, it was amazing that it hadn't happened sooner.

"You have a kind heart, Jackie." He sighed and led them to the elevator. "I just don't want you getting hurt again."

Neither did she.

After everything they'd been through, she knew their relationship was secure. The last thing he had left to worry about were her parents. More for her sake than anything else.

"I'm sure I can handle anything with you at my side." She pressed the button. As they waited she smiled impishly up at him. "Speaking of things bound to happen…"

His expression darkened, but he waited patiently for her to continue.

Jackie shifted from foot to foot. "You know how I promised nothing would come between us ever again?"

He glowered at her. "Yes."

When he tried to pull away she held him fast. So they were pressed so tightly against each other that nothing could get between them. "We need to make the most of this because when my stomach is out to here"—she stretched out her arm to demonstrate just how big it could possibly get—"it's definitely going to come between us."

Slack-jawed, Logan stared at her a long moment before a stupidly happy grin spread over his face. "You're serious?"

She nodded.

Logan let out a whoop, picking her up and swinging her around without a care about who saw. "I can't tell you how happy this makes me. It's incredible. *You're* incredible." He gently settled Jackie back down on her feet before cupping her cheeks and kissing her deeply.

He shuffled her in the instant the elevator doors opened and closed them before anyone else could enter.

"This calls for a celebration." Staring at the camera discreetly tucked in the corner, he pulled out his phone and quickly tapped on the screen. The little red light faded away just before he picked her up and pressed her to the back of the elevator. "Right now."

About the Author

Kait was born and raised in the wilderness of the Pacific Northwest and started writing as a child to entertain herself during the long winters. Insatiably curious with a love of learning new things, she's picked up many random skills including three languages and two martial arts. After traveling three continents (the other four are on her bucket list), she settled in England with her family where she spends most of her time cultivating her daughter's love of reading and writing, scribbling ideas on every available scrap of paper and trying out dialog on her cat.

Kait Gamble loves to hear from readers. You can find her contact information, website and author biography at http://www.totallybound.com.